To Natalie,

A very merry ...

Christmas Lovers

2016

Sarah Michelle Lynch

Thank you for taking Ade and David into your heart.

Sarah Michelle xx

ISBN: 1540730875
ISBN-13: 978-1540730879

DEDICATION

For the Lovers.

Also by the Author

A Fine Profession
A Fine Pursuit
The Chambermaid's Tales Pocket Sized
Unbind
Unfurl
Unleash
Dom Diaries
Fabien: A Vampire Serial
Angel Avenue
Beyond Angel Avenue
Tainted Lovers
Christmas Lovers
The Contract
The Fix
They Say I'm Doing Well
Break the Cycle

As S. M. Lynch:

The Radical
The Informant
The Sentient

ACKNOWLEDGEMENTS

Some of you may be surprised to know that *Tainted Lovers* was last year's Nano project. Then I had a book signing the following March and I endeavoured to get it ready for the event. So I never expected to receive such a variety of responses to the novel and it is your responses that prompted me to write this little number.

I hope this novella goes some way to reassuring you that even after all that happened, and beyond the amazing sex they enjoy, David and Adrienne are one soul.

I must thank Rachel Hague for her messages of horrified shock. I must thank her, along with all the other stalwart readers who stayed the distance with the original book. I cackled a little when you were all nearly throwing your Kindles, but I loved it when people wrote to me to say they completely got Adrienne in all her painfully real glory. Hopefully this little companion is a reward for you who stayed the distance.

I must thank the people who don't know me from Adam who write book reviews about my words. You are the ones who surprise me no end.

Thank you for reading.

Christmas Lovers

I neglect to mention that the story of my life with Adrienne is something I've written about... in secret... a story so heartbreaking, she could never write it herself, like I once suggested she might. Only I could write what for her was an unbearably sad time of her life. She was never black inside, whereas I am, and always will be. Which is why I could write our story, on her behalf, because I am the towering strength she clings to. Behind every beacon of hope, is someone like me, someone who can tell it like it is and get away with it for some reason. —*Tainted Lovers*

ONE

Christmas Eve Eve

It has been six months since we last had sex. That sounds bad but it's because I gave birth in June… and there's always the recovery after that, both mental and physical. The sleepless nights don't help. Hormone changes. Leaking breasts. There's bodily stuff you don't even want to talk to your doctor about, let alone your spouse. Between our jobs and looking after four kids, I think we've pinned all our hopes on tonight being the night we reconvene as lovers and I don't know about him, but I am tense. I do enjoy the annual work party but tonight it feels like a burden, an obstacle between us and the luxury suite awaiting us at Booth Castle hotel nearby. I could have declined the party invite of course but then we'd have had to tell my mother-in-law, our helpful babysitter, that we are only saddling her with four kids for the night because we need to have sex without fearing intrusion or the baby waking up crying. Besides, as I keep telling myself, this night is an important night for me professionally.

"Relax," he says, as the limo drives us towards Higham

Sands, a country house my firm has hired for the banquet.

I glance sideways. "How can you tell?"

"Your knee won't stop doing the fandango."

I look down at my knee. "Ah, you're right." I rub at it, trying to calm myself.

He reaches across the seat, takes my cheek and kisses the corner of my mouth. His tone is level as he tells me, "Everything will be perfect."

I'm not sure whether to air my grievances so I turn my face to look out of the window, deciding to remain quiet.

"Tell me what's going through that beautiful mind," he says, stroking his hand up and down my bare arm.

"I'm a bit nervous and, I don't know… it's just been…"

"Adrienne," he hums, taking my cheek. He pulls me towards him, his mesmerising brown eyes pinned on mine. "Kiss me."

I move across the seat slightly, take hold of his nape and brush a kiss over his lips.

Pulling back, I see his eyes are closed, his face expressionless. I worry this night is going to end in disaster. I worry… and I worry. I never used to worry about a thing.

He opens his eyes, grinning, his tongue flicking out briefly to taste his own lips where I just kissed him. "Adrienne, I know you've got yourself worked up, but this doesn't have to be the night, not if you're not ready. I'm so proud to call you mine, whatever. I'll wait because I love you, because I know it'll be beautiful when you're ready again. You're worth the wait."

"I appreciate you saying. God, I do. But it's not just that… it's…"

"You've been on maternity and you think they'll judge you?"

"I don't think, I know. I know from how they've treated female colleagues before. I'll be responsible for making other women in the company broody and more lost woman-power as more of us have babies and lose the company money… and… that's just how it works, we both know that. I'm enemy of the state number one right now."

"Tossers," he says, erupting with venom, "fuck the lot of 'em. Just quit, I don't care. Stay home. We have enough money! It's not worth you–"

"David!" I grab his wrist but he's shaking his head and determined to fold his arms. "As if I would be content with that."

"Well…"

I let the air between us cool before broaching the heart of the matter. "I would much rather we just went to the hotel and forgot the dinner but I just, can't. I've been working from home since David Junior was born and I feel as though I could regain respect by actually showing tonight."

"That's the most ludicrous shite I've ever heard sputter from your mouth!" he says, keeping his arms folded. "What are they? A bunch of out of touch, upper-class morons stuck in the Dark Ages?"

I burst out laughing, so hard my sides threaten to split. "YES!"

He takes my hand. "Let's play a game tonight, make it more fun? If we're to be subjected to the nonsense, let's make some of our own?"

"Go on…"

His eyes sparkle when he grins. "Every time anyone says the word funding, it really means fucking instead, at least in my mind. As in, 'I was trying to get the fucking for the development.' Or 'I was trying to get the fucking for my daughter to attend college in America.'"

"You twat, I'll hardly be able to keep a straight face!"

"And for good measure," he adds, "I'll be talking about funding for most of the night too, all the while knowing you're thinking about the funding as well."

I laugh, clutching his arm for support as I raise the roof off the limo almost. Wiping tears from my eyes, I don't say it but I think it:

What would I do without you?

I give him a deeper kiss than before and search his eyes as we near the venue, seeing only hope in his soul.

*

"You are so evil," I whisper in his ear as we stand in a quartet, alongside my boss and his wife. I work as a government regulator of mergers and acquisitions. I've recently been working on delivering a report about the merger of one of the UK's biggest food stores with one of the smaller ones. On the side I have also invested in future energy projects, something my father said was going to be huge business very soon. Every time I try to explain my job to David he nods off, which is funny really. People who aren't accountants or know about finance don't get accountancy or finance.

"You love my evil," he whispers back, his hand resting lightly around my waist.

Oh yes I do.

My boss, Mika Pietersen, grins in a slovenly, drunken way and asks in his strange Dutch accent, "So when are you coming back into the office, Adrienne?" No matter how many times I tell him to call me Ade, he ignores me – I think to annoy me.

I want to tell him that my boobs need to cease leaking before I return to work but I don't say that.

"Hopefully a little after Christmas, Mr Pietersen."

"I told you before, call me Mika."

I give him a look because until he calls me Ade, I'm not calling him his shortened version of his long forename either.

David clears his throat. "Everyone looks… good tonight. Especially Mrs Pietersen."

Mrs Pietersen, forename Alexandra, is a British aristocrat twenty-five years Mika's junior. She's practically just out of nappies. Alexandra blushes at David's words and I give him an evil, which only he sees. I despise it when he flirts with other women. Despise it! I can't abide it! Alexandra surely didn't marry Mika for his looks…

"I love your dress, it's so daring, so soon after having a baby," she tells me, in a passive aggressive way.

"I love it too," I reply, because I don't do bullshit exchanges.

"Let's grab canapés," David suggests, and we wheel over to another side of the room, me telling Mika as we go, "see you at the dinner table."

Alexandra gives me an envious look. She also hates that I have her husband's professional respect.

"That woman thinks I'm fundingly fundable, don't you think?" David says in my ear.

"You are so funding bad, you nerd."

"I love your fighting talk. Gets me raging hard."

"Oh shut up." I grab a canapé and shove it in his mouth. The look he gives me is one of amusement, despite almost choking.

Jerry and his husband Jeremy slide over towards us. Air kisses are exchanged all round. Just more people drooling over David. I am a jealous person and I can't help it. David's worth my jealousy. It would help if we could simply screw though. There's nothing that says a man still wants you like a good screw does.

"Did you hear funding is being cut in our department… yet again," says Jerry, or it could be Jeremy. I don't know. They're both dark and look like brothers almost. I've heard of people being attracted to other people who look like them, but…

"Ade told me that the funding cuts are going to be so hard next year," David interjects, and I swallow an annoyed, if amused, chuckle. "So, very deep, too."

I try to ignore his insinuation. "I truly didn't know if I would have a job to come back to after maternity leave."

One of them says to me in a sort of stiff, uptight way, "They can't. Imagine firing a woman just because she had a baby. You'd sue, they know that. Or make it national news."

"It happens all the time," David argues, "just in much more subtle ways. If Ade hadn't agreed to work full-time from home, Pietersen would have used the 'you don't have a place in this business anymore' card. It's bullshit if you think women don't have it tough."

"We're thinking of adopting," one of them says, I think Jeremy, but I'm not sure, "but we're terrified. Which of us would go on leave? Neither of us would like to drop that news on Mr P."

Jeremy and Jerry both work in M&A in the government contract sector, a section of the department quite separate to mine.

I look at David and I know what he's thinking without

even saying it. David's accountant has written this current tax year off as a research year, but really he's been looking after the kids. It turned out better than going on paternity, instead spreading around last year's royalties into this year's, so he's paying less tax this year, enough to make up the shortfall of not bringing out a new book in 2017.

"There's something about having your own kids," David says, "so why don't you try what Elton and David did? Mix the sperm. I tell you when you have your own flesh and blood in your arms, you don't worry about what paedo pricks like Mika might say for wanting to have your own kid and raise it in a healthy, loving environment. You somehow get through it."

Many people learn all too quickly about how little tolerance David has for procrastinators. He wrote several novels during his 'lost years' and many of them feature characters sat around waiting for life, probably how he felt at the time. He never painted those kind of people favourably – probably not very happy with his own choices at the time. Nowadays he doesn't waste a day. I work and he's constantly driving the kids around, to play dates and on trips out.

The two J's smile tightly, then kiss me, deliberately forgetting David.

"Catch you later, gorgeous woman," one of them says, the other one adding, "you look amazing."

"David…" I warn, giving him a look.

"Well, I can't fucking stand people who are shallow, going on about money all the time. It's funding stupid."

"Yes but we have loads of money, not everyone does."

"I know we have loads of funding to sort out later to fund ourselves into next week but at least our funding is real."

"You mean our funding produces babies?"

His face falls. "Hopefully never again."

"Then what the funding are you on about?"

He chuckles. "I don't funding know."

"Billy isn't your blood, but you've brought him up as your own?"

"Yes but he's half of you. And you belong to me. So it's different."

I shake my head at him. "I think someone would rather shake this lot off and go and get fucked… sorry funded."

We giggle together. I see our servers getting ready to ring the gong and lead us into the banquet hall. These things do go on for hours…

"I just see the bigger picture," he says, "like the fact that there are ordinary, working class couples out there who can't even scrape the money together for a round of IVF, and then they don't even know if it's going to work. Some people don't know they're born and this establishment you're a part of, well, it quite frankly smells of stale fart."

I laugh out loud. "Literally, too! We've fasted all week for this but I don't think many others have."

He grins, stroking my hand. "I prefer mingling with writers, I guess. When we get together we talk about war and peace, good and evil, not whether Thing One or Thing Two is going to be the stay-home daddy."

I burst out laughing, again. "The wiry hair, right?"

"God yes. I cannot believe my reading this year has mostly consisted of Dr Seuss. I will have to rectify that forthwith!"

He hands me his champagne glass, explaining, "Seems ungentlemanly I know, but I expect to be boxed in at the dinner table so I'll go potty now, rather than unceremoniously excusing myself at the dinner table, something ladies can get away with, not us."

He begins walking away when I retort, "It's decided. I'm hiring a nanny because my husband is becoming fond of potty."

He smirks over his shoulder.

"God, damn David," I say to myself, watching his immaculate arse stride away. He is still so gorgeous and unchanged and yet there are bits of me that have changed considerably, especially since David Junior weighed a whopping nine and a half pounds.

"Adrienne?" I hear a voice to the side of me.

Turning, I find myself staring at one of the firm's notorious cougars. It escapes me why she's waited for David to disappear before inviting herself over to talk with me.

"How's life?" I dare ask.

"Well, funding's being ripped to shreds again," Katrina says, and I endeavour to keep a straight face, "Mika would tear us a new one if he could, you know? He doesn't give a shit about the little people, just wants all the funding for his own fucking ends."

Mika, our section Head, is her ex-husband...

I put David's little game out of my head and try to show her sympathy. "I guess they're more concerned with keeping UK businesses afloat right now, than contracting in or out."

"My arse," she says, ready to combust, "more like he's got some mates high up in parliament."

I try to smile. "If it's any solace, I despise his teenage lover. She complimented my dress in a less than genuine manner... but I guess she has nothing better to say."

Katrina laughs. "You're so sweet, Ade. But your dress is lovely actually and such a pert arse for someone so thoroughly... what's the word?"

"Mumsy? Erm…" I try to think of a word, "…ripe?"

"Fucked," she says, "which is more than I am right now. Someone who's had four must have known a lot of fucking, yes?"

"Yes and no," I say, not wanting to pour all my secrets at once.

David returns to my side and shakes her hand. "Katrina, how goes it?"

"Better now," she says, with a slight wink. "You know, one of the new typists I was just talking to said that she's seen you before. But she couldn't possibly be right?"

His hand in mine turns hot. "I don't think so, Kat."

Kat, as he calls her, sometimes comes over to stay at our house if we are working on a joint project. Sometimes Mika makes us share the workload, because the funding is constantly being cut. It'll be a wonder if my husband's manhood survives this evening…

"I thought so, too. It couldn't be true." Katrina bites her lip.

"What is it? What are you hiding?" I demand of her.

She peers at me. "The girl I spoke with said she'd seen David in a porn movie. A high-brow one, she said, but a porn movie nonetheless. It went to DVD and everything. It's her favourite, she tells me. Her batteries run out regularly because of you, David."

David takes a deep breath beside me. "She's wrong, I must have a doppelganger, although I do have a cousin on my dad's side who looks exactly like me…"

Katrina laughs, a little manic-sounding. "What was worse was that the girl seemed to think you were one of those horrid, controlling dominants in the film. You know? All belts and chains and whips. One of those imperious bastards who force women to their knees. I mean, for god sake! As if you would do that. Even if it was in a film, it's just not you! Not the family man we all know and love."

While I glance at David beside me, red-cheeked, I feel like all my blood has seeped into my toes and wants out, the stuff holding me together determined to end me tonight out of shame.

The gong for dinner finally bloody rings and I'm now not even hungry.

"Lovely to see you two," she says, with a cheeky grin, knowing exactly what naughtiness she's caused, "I won't tell…"

David tries to hold my hand as we go through but I snap my hand back.

No way are you getting any tonight, I want to say.

I really don't need this.

Not right now.

Not when this was supposed to be romantic!

For god sake…

TWO

I'm utterly disgusted and absolutely mortified. At the dinner table finally, we're only sat opposite the girl who allegedly saw David in a porn movie! When she catches sight of him so close up, she actually begins pouring with sweat and drinking vast amounts of water.

"I want a seat somewhere funding else," I demand of my husband.

"Look at the place, we're packed in as it is. No way are they gonna let us swap seats now, not when allergies have been accounted for and all our menu choices stamped on the backs of the waiter's heads, otherwise we could have blow-fish city on our consciences tonight. I'm told the first course is bouillabaisse and Mika has a fish allergy. He could be hospitalised tonight if we move."

"Funding fund," I groan, and realise I better just deal with it.

Trouble is I don't even want to flirt with David to make her squirm.

So maybe I'll just make him squirm instead…

He holds up his hands. “Just gossip I heard at the urinals, that’s all.”

“I told you not to use those but use the cubicles. You always get blokes trying to look, as if they know… like they think they know… and they want to confirm it.”

David strokes a long finger up the length of my arm, from the inside of my wrist to my shoulder.

“There was a queue for the cubicles. It sounded as though Jerry and Jeremy were practising baby making. Look at them…”

I look down the table and realise David’s right! They’ve been screwing in the bathroom before dinner.

“They wouldn’t!”

“An amuse-bouche, perhaps,” my other half suggests.

“Quite frankly, I have never done such a thing before in my life!” I protest, for the benefit of any weak-hearted Christian earwiggers nearby, but when David’s hand squeezes my thigh under the table, I remember that I have – many times, of course.

As I peer across the vast divide of the large banquet table, I notice Little Miss ‘I Watch Porn All The Time’ (something else I’ve never done, of course), is staring at every, single little move he makes, like she can’t believe her fantasy is really real. The table garland and all the dinnerware around us won’t stop me from leaping over and killing her if she so much as smiles in my husband’s direction.

For fund’s sake.

“This is mega uncomfortable.”

“Then think how it feels for me,” he says quietly, “your genitals aren’t the ones she’s thinking about.”

I have a giggle to myself, but then I drop my tone, “I’m not buying it. I’m the wronged one here.”

The fish soup arrives but the girl doesn't touch hers, her starry eyes still fixed adoringly in David's direction.

"Excuse me, have we met?" I holler across the table.

She looks stunned that I am even addressing her, tongue-tied perhaps. Shaking her head briefly, she finally tears her eyes off our side of the table and stares down into her appetite-whetting soup.

"Be nice," he goads in my ear.

I'm going to ignore him.

"Do you know Katrina? She says you know David, apparently," I have to shout almost, over the din of people clanking their spoons, gnashing on their bread rolls and talking codswallop as they enjoy yet more champagne.

The girl colours completely, beetroot red from top to toe I would imagine.

I don't think she imagined Katrina and I to be friends. How could she know? Kat and I only work on rare projects together because we're in very different games. Maybe she thought Katrina doesn't have a big enough mouth to go blabbing about porn… clearly she bloody well has!

As I spoon my soup the proper way, because I've been brought up all proper, I watch her out of the corner of my eye. Beside me David huffs, subtly shaking his head. I've embarrassed her, obviously.

The unknown, nameless girl attempts to tackle her soup but fails. A colleague sat next to her briefly asks, "Not your thing?"

Unknown Porn Girl shakes her head, then lowers her eyes again. Her friend next to her gets back to talking to some random guy she clearly wants to have buried inside her later tonight.

For some reason I can't help thinking about why I used to

watch porn…

Maybe the girl's lonely, or at a juncture in her life where she can't take reality. It's been ages since David did porn so I'm thinking… this young girl might have stolen a video from her parent's private collection and kept it. So, he's found himself a true fan finally. A fanatic even.

"In the films," I say, keeping my voice down, "why are you always so commanding? I noticed it in some of your others."

He turns his head and stares. "Seriously? We're going to have this talk now."

I shrug.

He considers his answer before giving it to me. "Isn't that what women want? In the bedroom anyway."

I purse my lips. "Yes, but–"

You're not like that with me, not always. I want to say it, but don't.

He takes a strand of my hair, tucks it back behind my ear and strokes my cheek. "You look so beautiful tonight."

I smile a little, staring into his deep, brown eyes. "Will we ever forget the past?"

"No," he says, "but I think that's the point. It made us who we are now."

"And who are you?" I smile, chewing through a chunk of soda bread.

"Whatever you want me to be." He sounds so honest, I wonder…

"I want you to be you," I intone, "that's all I want."

I look up from my bowl, my soup demolished, to find the girl has done a runner – gone while I was distracted by David. Scanning the room, she's nowhere to be seen. Poof, into thin air she went…

I wonder if it was embarrassment or necessity that prompted her exit…

*

The dance floor is crowded despite us all being stuffed, lethargic and dazed. That humongous dinner ruined most of us. I'm glad neither of us have to drive home tonight. David tries to mask a burp against my shoulder and I chuckle. "Sorry, it was the Beef Wellington, I think."

"Or it could have been the cheese, or the fish, or the lamb skewers… who knows?" I press my face into his chest to disguise my own wind.

How romantic…

What is nice though is just being able to hold my husband without fear of anyone else stealing him away or looking at him as if he's a steak dinner.

"Love you," I mumble, resting my cheek against his shoulder.

"Do you want to go?" he asks, kissing the top of my forehead.

"I'm happy, just like this."

I really am pleased just to be dancing with my husband in peace for once. There are no kids trying to climb him, no kids for me to hose down, not to mention this is the first night in weeks he hasn't been wearing the lipstick that our two girls insist on painting him with all the time.

Dancing in hold, his thumb caresses the back of my hand and his chest moves against mine gently, his rhythm sure and steady, not exaggerated. I can barely even hear the music pumping out from speakers all around, I'm lost to the bliss of my husband, in a suit, smelling of linen and cologne, not sick or that horrible nappy smell you can never escape.

I'm floating.

I could fall asleep as he guides me around, our moves taking us nowhere near anyone else. All the socialising earlier and nonsense over dinner dispensed with, I'm finally languid and at peace.

For a moment I wonder if he's slipped me a pill or something because I feel uncharacteristically unworried. Rachel will be okay with the kids, I know, plus Rachel's new husband is a doctor so if any of them go skateboarding off the staircase or something, he'll be there to help them out.

I realise the sudden difference in the way I feel isn't down to any pill, or the luxurious meal or the amount of champagne I've had, it's that David is entirely calm now and it makes me calm when he is. As long as he's calm, I know there is nothing at all to worry about.

A finger taps on David's shoulder and it's Mika and his teenage lover. "We're going Adrienne. The missus has a bad case of stomach ache."

The girl does look rather peaky. Must be pregnant.

"I'm really glad we came," I tell him, "it's been a crazy year."

Mika, for all his faults, is an emotionally intelligent man and reassures me, "Don't think about a return to the office quite yet. We'll schedule you to pay a visit mid-January and we'll talk properly, lay all our cards on the table."

"That would be amazing," I gush.

"David," he says, and the pair shake hands.

"Hope you feel better," I tell Mrs Pietersen, whispering so Mika doesn't hear as he exchanges pleasantries with David, "and congratulations."

"Thank you," she says, looking green.

"It gets better, trust me."

She manages a tiny smile. "I hope so."

As Mika steers her from the building, David and I recommence dancing, but this time I wrap my arms around his neck so we can talk. "I think we've been mean about her."

"Why?"

"Maybe Kat didn't want to give him kids, but the young girl does."

He shakes his head slightly, tugging me closer so I can feel his hips, warm and firm against mine.

"How could you tell?"

"I've been there four times. I can tell."

"About that..."

I frown. "Oh...?"

I'm immediately on the defensive, wondering about the apprehension in his eyes.

When he smiles, he reassures me, "We don't want any more, do we?"

"No. Well, I know you would love it if it happened by mistake... but..."

"Then we agree, it might be best for me to get the snip. It'll save us a load of heartache. I know the pill is no good for you so I'm happy to do it, take the worry away. Make it possible for us to screw as much as we want, without worry, for the rest of our lives."

What he didn't say there was that the pill exacerbates my anxiety and depression. I've been lucky with David Junior. I haven't had any episodes yet but I know that post-natal depression could strike anytime. It's why I work and why David takes care of the kids. It sounds ludicrous but work keeps me sane. The job David does (staying home) is much harder than the one I do. Tonight proved that the world of commerce and enterprise and all that is a fickle game really. Funding comes and goes, but love and life, that's eternal.

"That's settled then?"

"If you're sure."

"I'm sure," he says.

I smile. "Thank you."

We kiss, touching lips lightly, and I pull back to see his eyes full of fire.

"You're the most handsome man here tonight, and that's not me being biased."

He delivers a smouldering stare, searching my eyes, my face. "And I nearly ruined our evening."

It doesn't fill me with pride that David had a varied and sometimes vacuous life before he met me.

It does however fill me with pride that he overcame so much to be here with me right now.

"You never talk about that with me," I say, braving a question, "why?"

He looks like he feels accused. "It's not who I am, just what I did."

"The girl sat opposite tonight, she looked at you as though you were that character you played in the films, David Dare. As though she believed you and he are the same… moreover, that he's real."

My husband takes a deep breath, his chest expanding so it swells against mine. I pull back slightly to give him air to breathe, hoping for an answer.

"Was it difficult for you to switch on that character?" I badger him.

He bites his lip, quashing the answer. His eyes admit it, his mouth won't.

"Just talk to me," I whisper, "I'm not going to change my mind about you, not now!"

He looks shy, and out of the blue, he chuckles. "God, you are an amazing woman. Even tonight, in the most diabolical of circumstances, you smile and throw around sarcasm, and even want to help me shave away the shame of my past."

"I'm not ashamed of you," I retort immediately, letting him know it's not that, "but there's still a part of you untouched, I feel it. I feel like the shame you feel is keeping me from a corner of who you are beneath, the whole you."

He swallows hard, barely able to look at me. He turns his face to the side. "Please, drop it now Ade."

"The wild man I know is under there, he's constantly hiding from me. Why?"

He looks uncomfortable, shaking his head. "I'm not enough then?"

I pull him closer, wrapping my arms tighter around his neck. Lifting my mouth to his ear, I whisper, "One day you came into the office at home… your shirt sleeves rolled up, vomit on your collar, a mad look in your eye as you tried to find Marissa's blankie. I heard her screaming downstairs and you grabbed the blankie from the day cot in my office, then left. I had to touch myself at my desk because you seemed so wonderful, to me. Nothing you could say or do could put me off. I'm still mad for you. Thirteen, almost fourteen years on, I'm madder than ever in fact."

He pulls me out of his shoulder and looks into my eyes. "I will never do what he did to you. I will never become like him. I'm here to protect you, remember?"

There are tears in the corners of his eyes. I see he's protected me from the wolf buried deep inside him, because he always sensed I was a battered woman.

"I love you so much, David," I gush, leaning up for a kiss.

He slides a hand under all my hair and holds the back of my head as he delivers a taunting, torturously delicate kiss, one strong enough to make my knees weak. His tongue merely fluttering against mine, I envisage that tongue all over me tonight.

"I'm ready to meet David Dare," I tell him, "I'm more than ready. I trust you completely."

David cuddles me close, stroking my face, the dance floor thinning now, the doors shutting soon. The car will be here any moment and it feels as though it will be a moment to remember, the minute we leave this hall and return to the hotel, renewed. Reawakened. Ready to submerge ourselves in one another again.

I can hardly wait for that moment but I'm also dazzled by his eyes. His anticipation. His reluctance, too. His confliction. His enormous sexual energy. How could I possibly let this man cut off his ability to produce babies when he produces such lovely children? How could I ask him to risk his manhood? I must be mad. I think I am. I think I want lots more unprotected sex with this man, without another big bump in the way.

"Don't I satisfy you enough? We've done a few crazy things throughout our married life. Experienced all kinds of sexual encounters. Can't you accept I'm happier being like this, being safe?"

I shake my head, side to side. "I am more than happy with you. I'm besotted with our life," I argue, "but I've always known there's another side of you and now, I'm desperate to meet him. I think you're desperate to let him out. Don't tell me you haven't had your hand around my gorgeous cock throughout this drought. Don't try to tell me you don't fantasise about tying me up and licking every inch of my body."

He appears stunned and as I press myself against him, hard.

"I'm your wife and I'm telling you, I want my David Dare, all night long."

He nods slowly, still unsure of himself. When his phone beeps with a text, letting us know our limo's here, he guides me from the room, nerves setting in for the both of us.

In the back of the limo, all I want is to take off my dress, let him lick me and fuck me until I can't see straight. He's fighting his urges too, desperate to touch me, I can tell. It's not like we haven't screwed in a limo before, but I sense his thoughts have escalated to acts he simply can't perform in a limo.

They must be performed in secret…

THREE

David pushes the key in the door and turns it slowly, giving me a sly smile over his shoulder. At forty years old, I don't think he's ever looked more beautiful, nor more self-assured. I simply can't express my love for this man in words. I'm hoping that tonight, he'll let me show him my love with submission. It's what I've secretly wanted for many years.

As we walk inside the hotel suite, I decide there couldn't be a better setting for this tonight. There is nowhere more beautiful, nor more luxurious. A former stately home, this castle hotel oozes comfort and glamour, large gilt mirrors all around making the chandeliers appear even more sparkly. The wood-panelled walls will protect us against the cold, not to mention there's a fire roaring in the large, open fireplace of our huge boudoir for the night.

I giggle, wandering the room at leisure.

"What?" he asks, sounding as calm as me.

I smile, stroking my hand along the silk covers on the four-poster bed. "I could be a princess, and you my prince. This place is amazing. I won't ever want to leave."

He gives me a knowing smile, standing by a side table where an ice bucket sits, chilling a bottle of champagne. "Adrienne, we can come back, perhaps anniversaries… birthdays… next Christmas?"

The corks pops and my senses with it. I don't want to feel anything but him tonight.

As he pours the champagne, I ask, "Where… moreover… how, would you like me?"

He walks to me, handing me a flute. We drink champagne how the Europeans do and then he tells me, "I want to talk first. I would hate to rip off such a beautiful gown prematurely."

He gestures at the two leather tub chairs by the fire and we walk together to the sitting area.

By the fire, I feel my cheeks absorb the heat and butterflies ricochet around my stomach. He seems mesmerised by the flames, licking and twirling at nothing, small amounts of dust and smoke barrelling up into the furnace.

"I want you to quit," he says after a while, turning his head slightly, his eyes on mine.

He looks intent, and possessive, and his stare tells me more than he's willing to vocalise. I know that me working isn't what he wants.

"I know."

He seems surprised I'm willing to admit it, just like that.

Turning his eyes back to the fire, he remarks, "They're not our people."

"No, they're my people."

"Adrienne…"

He only ever calls me that when he's feeling in a contemplative, odd mood. When my doctor of literature gets to thinking about things in a deep way, it's hard to yank him out of his own maudlin spell. It's strange that he's the dark one and yet, I needed him to pull me back into the light. I guess I never could cope with the dark and when the dark pulled me in, it was he who saved me.

"I could relapse," I tell him, "anytime. We both know that. I feel lucky, really. Luckier than most. I didn't take pills while carrying David Junior and I am on a low dose now. I feel okay but we both know, I could go back."

"You won't," he stresses, an argumentative tone buried deep in his annoyed demeanour, "when you broke down before, it was different. There was so much out of your control, out of our control, but this time it's different."

I sniff. "You think I'm burying myself in work?"

"Aren't you?"

I swallow. "Maybe. I don't know."

I roll my shoulders because my neck feels tight.

"Adrienne," he coos this time, and I lift my eyes to his.

"Hmm?"

"They offered me loads of money for film rights," he pauses, hating to say the next words, "for… *Chasing Delilah*, and they want me to write the screenplay. I can't do that while I have four kids needing me every five seconds."

I sense much. "You've been scared to tell me?"

"I know you hate *that* book," he admits, regret passing over his face.

That book more than vaguely resembles our story. I've yet to read it because I already know I'll hate it. In the summer he published *Chasing Delilah,* the story of a battered woman whose only exit was to kill her lover… only for his brother to come after her later down the line. David wrote it under a pseudonym but I still can't bear to think of the fact that it exists. I still worry his agent will spill the beans about the book being based in reality. I worry David Lewis's readers might one day spot a similarity in language use or style between his crime books and *Chasing Delilah,* more a romantic thriller.

I'm trying not to show him how this makes me feel. I keep my lip biting to a minimum, pressing my mouth together, but I can't help how I feel.

"We could get a nanny to cover for you then, while you write the screenplay. Remember that girl I used to have?" I squeeze my eyes shut, because of course he doesn't remember – he was seemingly dead when I had that nanny. "She was great. I'm sure there are others out there."

"Adrienne," he demands, "why don't you want to be alone with the kids?"

I swallow the huge globule of fear in the back of my throat. "In case I lose it one day. That cannot happen, not in front of my kids."

He nods fast. "I understand but that was all so long ago now. You're doing so well and you know in yourself the triggers. You're tooled up. This isn't like before, we're now no longer trapped in that web of Luca's. We're free."

"I'm not free, David," I argue, draining my champagne, "I know I'm sane, yes. Right now, I am. But sometimes, I can be in the shower, or in the garden, or changing a nappy and I blink… then in the next moment, I see him. He's on the ground. The gun's still smoking. My mother's dead. My life, is destroyed. Everything, is gone. It's like I'm right back there and do you know what? My mind might be fixed but my heart never will be."

He puts down his glass on a side table and kneels by my side. Against the light of the fire, his eyes shine more fiercely than I've ever seen them shining.

He looks up into my eyes, a man worshipful, desperate. "Come with me, Adrienne. On our next adventure. Come with me."

"Where are we going?" I ask, but I already have a sinking feeling. "You're just writing the screenplay?"

He lowers his head, looking at the floor. "The money would mean we never have to work again, but to market the film, it might need to become known that it's based on true events, that it's not entirely fictional."

"No." It's a simple response. No way. There's no leeway here. "Just no."

"I'd go and be on set, oversee everything. I've worked on sets before, and the producers like that. My agent is going to throw a load of contracts around to force people to keep their mouths shut but I said if I sell, I need to have creative control and therefore I need to be there."

"People will know," I spit, "your poor mother, my dad! Oh god! My dad!"

"We'd have closed sets and my nom de plume is tight, our real names kept out of it. Don't you see? This could really work! A Hollywood film!"

"No."

"I'll even stay away from the promo."

"No."

David shoots me disappointed eyes. "I knew you would be dead against this, but don't you see?"

"I see that you're an obnoxious prick when you want to be." My words sound cold, entirely as intended.

I stand and walk around the room, annoyed. How could he spring this on me now? Tonight? When it's meant to be *our* night for becoming lovers again.

"You don't see that this could be a really great film, inspiring others."

"I wouldn't wish my life on anyone, fictional or otherwise. I cannot believe how insensitive you are! Making money from my pain! How dare you? How dare you! It was bad enough you write it and then stick a fictional spin on it… but… this? My god!"

"With the money, we can travel, take the kids. Retire early. Set up charities. Do whatever. Never set the alarm clock again. Work when we like. The possibilities are endless."

"We have enough money," I argue, "and you are talking about a fantasy."

"But this is my dream," he musters, and I turn and look at him, still knelt on the floor, still begging.

"What?" I gasp. "What dream?"

He takes a visible deep breath, stands and walks to me, holding my elbows. "To write, then make a film. To make something powerful, something great. I want the whole world to know how proud I am of you."

A lump in my throat, I shake my head. He should have been a diplomat.

"Billy's already knee-deep in his GCSEs."

"He could stay with my mother to finish his exams but the girls and Davy, they can come with us and Billy can catch up."

"Where are we going?" My voice is but a whisper.

I hate that he seems to have this all figured out already.

"They want to shoot in Scotland, and also Italy, you know?"

For the scenes there…

"I want to oversee this. It's my life's work, I know it."

I grind my teeth. "Your life up until now?"

"I guess." He shrugs.

"And what about my life's work?" I feel wronged, and when I park myself back in the tub chair, I do so with a loud thud. "Do you remember how hard I worked to get where I am now? Do you remember the sacrifices I had to make?"

He walks away, annoyed, heading for the champagne bottle.

He pours more for both of us, seating himself opposite me once more.

"I just wanted to have sex tonight and you bombard me with this bollocks!"

"I don't get it," he mutters, his brooding eyes fixed on the fire so they can't hurt me, "you want me to be domineering in the bedroom, but everywhere else, I have to ride shotgun."

I suck in a deep breath, keeping my cool. I know I could destroy him with just a few words. David is so sensitive beneath, just a boy really, desperate for love.

"My work keeps me sane, I admit. But this is more than just a change, it's a risk. It's normal for me to feel afraid," I argue, covering my eyes with a hand. "I also don't believe it does anyone well to linger on the past and on a past so dark and dangerous, to boot. How can we go back over all of this, again? It feels like we'll never be free of it. I don't think we have the right to make money from something so disgusting." I throw my hands up. "I got it with the writing, yeah…that's an expression for you, an outlet… a sort of therapy… but with this film, it'd be like we're fucking milking it."

"I'm not afraid," he tells me authoritatively, "of anything. Anything but losing you. But this, this is a life-changing thing, you know? An once in a lifetime opportunity. Why do you think I want creative control over the cock suckers who would sanitise this, huh? If I do do this, I'll get iron-tight creative rights. I won't have it whitewashed."

"I wish you'd told me before tonight, rather than ruining my mind with this now, when we're meant to be here for a romantic evening."

"You have to put your faith in me," he begs, "trust in my judgement, know that I will take care of you, no matter what. I love that you are so conscientious but you have four beautiful children who worship you and want you to join us on trips out. You have so much beyond your career. A career you can keep, a career you don't have to say goodbye to completely. I'm not going to stop you looking into investments and whatever else you want to do, but you can take advantage of me, I really don't mind. Moreover you can take advantage of the liberties offered to us because we've worked so hard to get where we are now and for just a few minutes, you can take a breather and relax. I'm asking you to do that, for me. It will make me so happy to see you surround yourself in stuff other than spreadsheets for a while."

I grin, I can't help it. "But I do love my spreadsheets."

"I know, Ade. But there is nothing I love more in this world than you and I want to take care of you and our family. I want to do that by making you see, you're strong enough now. I want you to finally accept that you deserve happiness, because you do. You deserve all that and more. Let me make you happy."

Tears sting the backs of my eyes. "I love you so much but please see how hard this is for me–"

"I know." He leans over, elbows on knees, and reaches for my hands to kiss them.

Everyday I wake and fill my mind with tasks to do, numbers to crunch, errands to run. Sometimes what I forget to do is work on me. On my guilt. My regret. My fears.

"Let me take it all away from you," he begs again, softly whispering, "if we're going to do this, you have to trust me one hundred per cent, in everything. I want your whole faith, in me. I want it all Adrienne. I'm all or nothing, you know that."

I reach forward and tug him closer. He topples to his knees before me, looking up into my eyes again. I cup his face and smooth his cheeks.

"I'll try," I promise.

He threads all of his fingers between all of mine and kisses my knuckles.

"Nothing will make me happier than to be able to take care of you. I'll take great pride in it, very great pride in it," he says, his chest puffed out, his lungs working hard as he struggles to control his emotion, "it's my true life's work. Nothing else matters in comparison. Nurturing us and what we have, that's all that counts. All those people tonight Ade, what will they have to take to the next world? Possessions? Success? Us… we'll have a love so strong, it will carry us together forever. We'll never be apart. I'm tied to you, remember?"

A tear loaded with passion and love leaves my eye. So thick with emotion, it splashes on my forearm and stains my pink dress. "I remember."

He holds his hand on the side of his torso, where the tattoo he has resides, a tattoo corresponding to a similar one I have.

"No other achievement but us matters," he intones again, "and everything else, and everyone around us, benefits from us being happy. We're the centre of our own universe and protecting us, that protects everyone else. Don't you see?"

I nod. "I want to see."

He strokes my cheek, rising on his knees to give me a little kiss on the cheek.

"I'm just doing it for you, on behalf of you, because I love you."

"I need time with it."

"Time I can give. I'm okay with that."

"Okay…"

We hug it out and he kisses me quickly.

"Now, Adrienne. I bought you something which I left earlier in the bathroom. Even before we decided what this night would be, I knew that this little something would make you happy."

I feel a smile crease my face in a way I haven't been moved in months. "What is it?"

He grins, pursing his lips. "It's just something I saw and… I thought of you."

"I'm intrigued…"

He helps me from my chair, pushing me in the direction of the en suite bathroom.

"Be quick," he says, beginning to loosen his tie.

I feel like I'm being caught in a trap. Perhaps just this once, I'll allow him to lay waste to my controlling nature.

I'm desperate to know what he's been getting up to behind my back. How did he sneak in a surprise for me, in between changing nappies and scooping up sick?

I walk in and lock the door. I want privacy to assess what it is he's got for me.

Looking around the room, I don't immediately see what it is he's got for me. All I see are the toiletries we placed on the counter earlier after check-in, plus the usual bottles and complementary products hotels always provide.

"Hang on…"

I spot a note on the back of the door:

You're freezing cold over here.
What about on the counter?

I chuckle to myself and look amongst the bottles and tubs on the twin-vanity unit.

"What nasty surprise have you got in store for me, darling?" I say to nobody but me.

Among the bottles and the usual stuff we put on our faces or in our mouths everyday is a tub I have never seen before. On it, another note:

Smear me all over your bald pussy.
If it isn't bald, make it bald.
Stockings on. Bra on. Suspenders on.
Pussy dressed in chocolate.

I spot the spreading stick under the lid and almost burst out laughing, instead guffawing into my hand. It's lucky I had a wax a few days ago, in readiness of our special night tonight. He must have known I would be nervous about being intimate with him again.

God I love that man.

"How's it going?" he asks from behind the door.

I decide to lie. "I'm getting bald. Be patient."

"Okay…"

I hear him rustling in the champagne bucket again. I can just imagine him pacing the room in his trousers, shirt and cummerbund. I bet he looks funding fundable.

"Damn you, David Lewis."

Taking my zip to task, I manage to get out of my dress easily. Hooking the shoulder straps on the pegs of the door, I leave it hanging there so it doesn't get anymore creased.

"How could you do this to me, Lewis?"

I look at myself in the wide mirrors surrounding the large vanity units and wonder if I can follow through.

Okay.

I take a breath.

Then another.

First thing's first, I have to take my knickers off. Then cover myself with chocolate paste!

I drain the dregs of my champagne glass and readjust my tits in the balcony bra I'm wearing. My tits are in pain wearing this thing because I need to release some of my milk. I can hardly do that now, with pasting duties awaiting me.

I twang the straps holding up my stockings and thank my earlier self for choosing a thick suspender belt which covers most of my stomach. It's black. It's lace. It's demure. It's flattering. It covers the slightly saggy bits, or rather holds them firm.

My body has changed over the years but one thing that hasn't are my legs. David loves my long, long legs. I want to get in a time machine and kiss my teenage self for swimming, cycling and running, which have always given me good muscle memory to work with. I have good legs, so at least if the rest of me ends up sagging, I can roll those bits up and just use my legs as my best assets!

Staring into the mirror, I realise he's probably having too much fun out there. He's anticipating me coming out, having carried out his instruction. He's so sure he can control himself tonight, isn't he? Well, I might just be able to do something to make him lose control…

I remove my lace thong and hang that over the pegs on the back of the door too.

Feeling my skin below, I am so pleased I booked that wax. It left the skin feeling so smooth, the proverbial baby's bum sort of smooth, but even smoother. Like satin. Velvet. Like it's criminal to walk around with such a smooth, silky, wet pussy all the time.

Licking my lips, I stare at myself in the mirror.

The large suspender belt has helped hide my sins so well, as has the balcony bra which I rolled my tits into earlier. I do look good and more importantly, I feel good.

"Adrienne…" I hear, and, I know he sounds impatient.

"Just a few more minutes…"

Let him sweat!

I swipe my index finger through my slit and it feels so delicious, I almost want to stand here and masturbate myself. But I won't. I've waited so long for this, I don't want to spoil it. But oh, the feeling of wetness, peeking out from all my silky baldness… I know exactly how wild this will make him.

I take some wetness and dab it around parts of my body. At the sides of my throat. Tops of my breasts. Bum cheeks. Backs of my knees. Toes.

I'm practically dry again down below once I've scented myself enough to make him lose control of himself tonight. He thinks he can overpower me…

Let's see him try.

I lastly take the tub of chocolate paste and decide to become artful. Sitting on the side of the bath, I spread my legs and create a heart-shaped chocolate treat for him, covering all the little nooks and crannies of my petals and folds, the V of the love heart dipping into my slit, the big bulges at the top decorating where there would normally be hair.

"I'm ready," I say, warning him.

"I'm waiting."

"I have done as instructed," I say through the door, "only there might be a slight surprise."

"Yes?"

I throw open the door and stand before him, finding David sat waiting expectantly on the edge of the bed.

"I was bald already so I had a little extra time to plant surprises all over my body for you."

His breath catches in his throat.

"Get on your hands and knees and crawl to me," he demands, "slowly. And you better be warned, that naughty little ass is going to get spanked so good."

I bite my lip. "Have I been very naughty, Daddy?"

"You've been so naughty baby girl. I'm going to make you wish you were even naughtier…"

I get on my hands and knees and keep eye contact the whole time I crawl to him, slowly but surely.

"Daddy's ready," he warns, but I hope he hasn't forgotten how rebellious I can be at times.

FOUR

I'm kneeling, looking up into his eyes, awaiting instructions.

"I love your hair down," he says, surprising me. I would have thought he'd want me licking his cock by now. At the very least.

"It takes work," is my – hopefully – submissive response, "but I know you love it like this."

Usually I pin it up for work and for when I'm holding the baby, so at least he's not sick in my hair as well.

"I love every part of you, do you know that?" he remarks.

"I wish I loved every part of me."

"We can change that," he says, a calm in his eyes I've never seen before, "we can do anything, together."

"I'm willing."

All humour seems to have left the room again and I'm left with only my dark and serious man sat opposite.

"I want you to serve me tonight, in every way. You'll do everything I say."

"Everything?" I gulp.

"Yes."

"Okay…"

"Adrienne, you're a girl inside, a girl who needs her daddy. Tell me it isn't so."

I pout, blinking fast. It registers for about a second that this role play comes so natural to me, but then I forget it's play at all…

"I need my daddy."

He nods briefly, a smile reaching his eyes. "And does my baby girl want to do everything her daddy says?"

"Yes."

"And why's that?"

"Because I need love from my daddy… and acceptance. But more than anything, I need recognition of my achievements. I need rewards, I need to work and be rewarded. It's who I am. I want to make Daddy proud."

"And Daddy will show you that you can achieve… in ways you never imagined."

I nod in compliance.

"Now baby girl, I know you've been naughty in the bathroom. Did you touch yourself?"

I brave a look into his eyes. "I did but not to pleasure myself."

He smiles warmly, this man – the custodian of all my happiness, the one man never to use or abuse me. We hurt one another a long time ago… but that's all history now. It brought us right here, to this special night.

"Tell me," he simply asks.

"I wanted to test you so I daubed little amounts of my sexual pheromones around my body for you."

He tries not to show his glee.

"You wanted to test me?" His eyes invite me to spar with him.

"Yes."

"But, why?"

"Don't all men want to be tested?"

"Not this man."

I bow my head, worried now that I've upset him.

He lifts my chin with one, long index finger. "I was tested and I hope I passed those tests?"

I nod.

"Sorry, Daddy." I look to the side, ashamed for some reason.

"There is nothing to be sorry for. I don't need testing, not me. The one thing that makes me happier than anything else is to know I make you happy. I do, don't I?"

I look at the floor, trying to contain my emotion. "Very happy."

"Then let us openly explore how we make each other happy, like this. No tests. Just exploration of our love."

"Yes, Daddy."

"Now go into the bathroom, clean your juice off your secret places, and come back to me ready to give yourself whole… to me."

"Yes, Daddy."

I crawl back to the bathroom, his little kneeling princess, and I wipe my pussy juice from the various little places I hid it. To get rid of any dampness, I powder myself a little and as I'm working, I notice the chocolate paste has completely dried and sealed my sex shut. I wonder if he intended this.

Crawling back to him, I wait patiently for more instructions.

"Daddy needs a bath and then a bedtime treat."

"Yes, Daddy."

As he undresses, I watch the floor. I'm in character, too

shy to look at my masterful daddy in all his looming glory.

"You could never disappoint me," he says, and I nod.

While he walks to the bathroom wearing just his boxer shorts, I crawl on my hands and knees behind him, so thankful of the deep pile carpet beneath my knees.

He waits patiently as I begin running the bath, pouring salts in, and just a little foam too. Exactly how he likes it.

As the water warms, I tell him, "It's warm enough if you want to get in while I top it up."

He keeps his focus on nothing but my eyes.

My focus is on nothing but him licking the chocolate off. I can barely concentrate on a thing else.

"Thank you, baby," he says, removing his underwear and sinking himself into the bubbles.

Once the roll-top tub is fully filled and he seems at ease, I ask, "Shall I wash your hair?"

"Yes, baby girl."

I want to get in, sit behind him, wrap my legs around him and stroke my hands all over his muscular body. He still gets up every morning, carries out his routine of press-ups and sit-ups, sometimes a few other moves too. He's fitter than ever in fact because he rarely drinks and is always chasing after the kids.

Using a clean mug, I pour water through his brown hair and listen to him humming as I attend to him.

"Do you want my shampoo? As a treat. I know you like it."

"Go on, then."

I use my coconut shampoo on him, which is for blonde hair, but he loves the smell of it.

Kneading the product through the lengths of his locks, I wait until the foam thickens and begin washing it away.

"Conditioner?"

"Just this once. You're spoiling me."

"I like to," I say, because he rarely lets me.

Using a minimal amount of conditioner, I massage his scalp and he moans loudly. I must be doing it right.

"That's good?"

"So good. I have a slight wine headache. I only get it from drinking champagne you know."

"They make it so you don't remember how many glasses you've had," I murmur.

"That's right. I expect I drank lots trying to cope with the soullessness of the whole affair."

"I'll make Daddy all better."

"Yes, you will."

Without words I grab a washcloth and cleanse his back and shoulders, kneeling behind the tub, the marble floor a little harder on my knees in here. As I'm cleaning his face, I admire his features while his eyes are closed. He looks so edible, so ready for my lips all over him, his skin moist and supple, his slight stubble begging to scratch my soft skin.

"Come and stand in the bath," he asks, still with his eyes half-shut, "don't get your underwear wet though. Take off your stockings."

"But the belt–" I begin to protest.

"The belt can stay, if it pleases you."

I give a slight nod as he opens his eyes to watch me.

Unclipping the stockings, they begin to slowly slide down my thighs without help and then it is just a matter of me tugging them the rest of the way. I slide them slowly, watching him all the while. I wish I could see more of him but he's buried beneath bubbles and all that water the large bath can hold.

I step carefully into the tub, to where he plants me, between his open legs. He sits up, half of him emerging from the water, his chest hair sopping. Rivers run over his chest and back.

"How badly do you want me to break the seal on your pussy, baby?"

"Badly." I'm not ashamed to admit, the seal would soon break anyway, the dam unleashed. He leaves me breathless when he puts his hands on me.

"You have to promise me something," he says, as I remain precariously stood in the water, "you must not come until I say."

"Yes, Daddy."

His hands grip my heels underwater, his eyes flash with a hint of mischievousness, then his fingers glide up my calves, gripping my thighs as he gains more height on me.

I shudder against his passionate gaze, against his need and mine. Our combined lust takes my breath away as he pulls apart my thighs and kisses the front of my leg.

My lip trembling, I can hardly breathe. I've waited so long for this. So, so long.

Going without David's body is like asking the Queen to go without her handbag.

"I love you," I mumble, sounding like a crazy person.

I'm so emotional you could blow me down like a feather. I need all his strength now. I need him because the years have changed me. They've made me more frightened and vulnerable. Life has made me more insular and I want to be able to live again, but I am still so afraid. I fear I will need to go back to hospital, have my head re-examined and be forced to start from scratch again.

My mind's racing away with all these thoughts when he

interrupts, "Adrienne, stop thinking. I hear you thinking. Just stop. I'm going to kiss my gorgeous fucking wife and she's going to have to work very hard to stop herself creaming into my mouth the moment I finally get my tongue on her clit."

"Shit," I mutter, "shit."

When his hands grab my buttocks, I feel the need in him through his iron grip, his needy testament to how much he's missed me too.

"Such bad things, such bad, bad things," he utters, before he kisses my lower stomach, his kiss needy and forceful, tasting my flesh, my skin, long untouched. I don't care if I'm still baggy or if I'm marked, he needs me and I need him. We're each other's souls. There's nothing else I need worry about.

"Oh my love," I whisper, as he holds me, encircling me with wet arms, his cheek against my thigh.

"I've missed you so much, Adrienne."

"Me too."

He begins lapping gently at the chocolate covering my bald skin and the furnace buried behind the chocolate barricade begins to break through.

"You knew," I gasp, "the chocolate would dry."

"Yes, and I would have to hunt for my gift beneath…"

He takes tentative, slow, precise licks, as if a child again, licking the bowl or the spoon, knowing there'll be no more after it is all gone, so he knows he has to eke out the pleasure of enjoying something so rarely enjoyed, so rarely given…

I'm pulsating with lust, I can barely stand a second longer, and I hope he has a back-up plan. He takes my bum in his hands, guiding me, turning me, and I sit precariously on the highest edge of the bath where the neck rest is. Clutching the edge of the bath, I throw my head back and he kisses me, a greeting.

"Stunning," he whispers, lapping, edging, tasting, driving.

I can't think, only feel.

I forgot how delicate he can be, how knowledgeable he is of my likes and dislikes. He knows I hate teasing, I just want him there, touching me in whatever way he likes.

Every time I feel my muscles become overwhelmed I breathe deep and fast, holding off, keeping my orgasm at bay. I'd happily come any second now but he told me to wait.

"Resist," he reminds me, but I'm tempted to let go every time his tongue connects with my clit.

The heat inside me is building to burning, to seizing me beyond my control, my breathing erratic, painful, my control…

…gone.

"Oh god, I can't…"

I come. I can't stop myself. I'd come without touch anyway. I'm in a state of such arousal, my walls knead against the emptiness there and though I'm dripping and extremely aroused, I'm not sated because my body came against an emptiness.

He tuts, wiping his mouth. "Adrienne…"

"Don't be too hard on me, Daddy. I have gone without so long."

He narrows his eyes. "But you have been self-administering?"

I shake my head slowly. "No. I've just… it's just not been there, until now. The need, I mean. I don't know, I haven't felt sexy in so long."

Suddenly, without warning, he tugs me into the bath with

him, drenching my bra and suspender belt. Water spills over and crashes to the floor with a slap.

My eyes close against the feeling of him holding me, embracing me. Pure bliss, I can only try to absorb it while I have it.

While he's nibbling my throat, I unclip my bra and throw it over the side. He releases my suspender belt and that gets tossed overboard as well.

My arms tightening on his neck, he begins shifting me into position and then I remember…

"David, you need a condom."

"I know but I…"

"No, David. Remember the last time you said it would be okay… that was fifteen months and one baby ago."

"Bloody hell, Adrienne."

"I know," I gasp, tugging his hair.

"I should punish you and all shades but I'm bursting too…" He's shaking against me, clawing for more contact, for us to merge finally, as one again. "…I can't help myself."

"David, please," I beg.

He steps out of the bath, dripping with water. At the vanity unit he pulls a condom from one of the toiletry bags and rolls it on.

"Out, now," he demands.

I walk to him, then he throws me up into his arms, and slams me against a wall.

"I love you," he tells me, all gravel, and pushes against my soaked flesh, need engulfing me.

My thighs slipping against his, he pushes hard and manages to get deeper inside, my body not used to him, as though re-virginised.

"I'm…" I don't say it. I can't. If I say it, it will happen. I'll come.

I'm hot and ready for him again but knowing David, it will take him some time to get there. He can go for hours.

"Just fucking come," he growls, his earlier stance ripped up and torn to shreds, our lust having overtaken us.

Biting his ear, I let myself go, tugging on his body with my legs, pulling him tight into me as I let myself enjoy an orgasm while his penis is there to grip and pummel. God, it feels so good, I feel so full and I'm weightless now, nothing matters, nothing… it's all nothing…

He kisses my mouth, tongue lapping, licking, dipping, the contact messy and rough. He drags me back to the present, wanting, needing – his own release so close now.

He moves me from the wall to sit on the edge of one of the sinks.

I grab his buttocks, knowing he's almost… so… close. He'll be coming round the bend anytime.

"Permission to give you what you want," I tell him.

"Granted."

I've come hard already. I could come again, I know. However at this point I'm more than eager to earn some brownie points. Slipping off him and to my knees, I rip off the condom and slide my mouth over his cock, taking two hands to him as well.

"Jesus, Adrienne."

He puts one hand against the wall behind me to steady himself and I worship him. While my hands massage and twist, pumping and demanding, I lick his balls and grunt, "So hard."

Flicking my tongue against a particularly sensitive vein in the tip of his cock, he loses control, grimacing and panting, his chest puffing fast.

His hips throw forward and he spurts against my lips, down my hands, and all over my arms. I catch what I can, never having particularly liked the taste of cum, though there's something special about tasting the man you love.

I kiss his abs, travel up past his breastbone, to his Adam's apple, drawing myself up onto my feet again. Tugging me into him, he stares into my eyes, the storm of his love not abated but only stirred inside him. He'll want me again now, having tasted our long-forgotten passion, our hunger for it only refreshed.

"We should fuck like this everyday," he growls, as I roll my forehead over his moist chest.

"So good, I agree." We should fuck like this every day, but life… it has a habit of getting in the way.

With a delicate kiss to my lips, he says, "Bathe with me."

We dip ourselves into the bath together and I wash him in silence, my legs wrapped around him. I can't stop smiling as he lies in my arms but something dark in him has risen again and he seems stern and determined.

"What next?" I ask as I pull the plug.

"I haven't decided yet," he says, and I know he's being honest, and I know that whatever he does with me next, it'll be good, if not great.

FIVE

We're by the fire in our hotel robes, made of luxury Turkish cotton. The material's so soft it hardly absorbs, even though it's a towelling robe. David lounges in one of the tub chairs while I sit at his feet, my cheek against his bare knee. One of his legs is thrown over the arm of the chair but he's strategically placed his robe so I can't see the loveliness between his legs. In my hand I hold an Irish coffee. David ordered two to be brought up to the room after we finished our bath. I sense he hasn't done with me, nor will he be done with me tonight. He knows coffee keeps me up all night.

"What do you think that girl sees in Pietersen?" he asks.

"Money."

I catch him frowning. With one hand he's holding the glass mug containing his drink and with the other, he's playing with my hair.

"Just money?"

"Maybe he's tender behind closed doors. Maybe attraction doesn't always have to fit a mould, you know? Two beautiful people… rich man, slim wife. Seems so boring really, doesn't it? Maybe fat and thin attract, young and old, rich and poor, stupid and super intelligent… maybe souls don't have a status in this world and souls attract for reasons beyond our knowledge."

I look up at him and he laughs, which makes me laugh.

"Adrienne, as tender as your words are, I don't imagine he's tender at all. He used to be married to Kat. I mean, I doubt she wanted sensitive. She's a cougar, remember? Didn't you tell me she often collars guys to do her up the bum on her lunch break."

I snicker. "God she's terrible isn't she, but it's absolutely true. I once caught her!"

David sighs, still stroking my hair. It feels so good to be by the heat of the fire and I feel so much more relaxed since finally getting some.

"Maybe Kat emasculated him, overrode him," I say chuckling.

"You do have a way with words tonight, dear."

"So he picked a younger model second time round, someone who surely wouldn't try to ride him like a derby horse."

David chuckles. "You can ride me how ever you like, anytime. I could never be emasculated. If anything it empowers me to see you take pleasure from me."

I look him dead in the eye, seeing curiosity there. "I know you don't like Mika but is there something else? You seem to have brought him up into conversation for a reason."

He smiles but it quickly fades, unable to hide his true thoughts from me.

Biting his lip, he then swallows hard. "I'm sure I heard him and Kat in the stalls of the work's party tonight…"

I press my lips together. "But his wife's pregnant?"

It dawns on me that there was a time when I was pregnant and everything went to shit and David used another woman because he couldn't handle the problems we were having…

I sense David has brought this issue up on purpose, because he wants to tackle it, even though it's history now.

I stare at the fire.

"He might be staying with her because she's pregnant. It might still be Kat he really loves, or maybe the wife is the one he can stand to live with, and Kat's the one he can't stand to live with but loves to fuck."

"I don't know…" I don't like talking like this. David becomes so analytical sometimes. "…I wish I understood men better. I feel sorry for the girl, she's young and doesn't know better. She would probably forgive and forget for the sake of the child."

"Adrienne, I often wonder how we've stayed together. Sometimes I wake up and it all seems a mirage. I don't think I deserve you. I mean I know I don't, and I still imagine you'll wake up one day, realise I'm a total and complete bastard, and you'll leave me."

"Like I said, husband," I intone, with plenty of sarcasm, "souls don't have any regard for worldly shite, souls love other souls on instinct and deep, simplistic compatibility. Our eyes met across a room and sparked a whole life we've now built together. A split second and my life was changed forever. I think without even knowing it, in those first few instances, we'd already recognised in each other a black soul. But then life in its irony threw us a curveball and it was needing the fairytale that actually fucked us up. If we'd stopped trying to hide our true selves from the beginning, we'd have been okay."

"You mean if we'd have just laid our cards on the table at

the same time, we'd never have gone through all we did."

"Yes." I keep staring at the fire because the fire absorbs my fears and my residual heartache, a type of agony that might never go away.

I'm in love with a man. He just also happens to be the same man who hurt me more than anyone else on earth. I guess that's the risk you take when you love someone so deeply – you leave yourself open to getting hurt.

"I wrote you a new poem," he says, "but it's at home. I can recite it for you, though?"

"Okay," I reply softly.

David's poetry is his way of telling me things he finds hard to say in simple terms. He's a wide galaxy of complex emotions and I'm still discovering things about him all the time. Like for instance the other day, I found out he loves peanut butter sandwiches. I never knew because he never said and I've never bought it because I hate it and the only reason I found out was because Billy needed a batch of peanut butter sandwiches making up for an American-themed party he was throwing. I almost threw a fit at the thought of a nut-allergy causing chaos but that's what they wanted. Anyway…

David closes his eyes and using his photographic memory, recalls the poem for me…

"I take thy enthusiasm
Into my heart,
Your interest
Into my soul.
You see something,
Read something,
I might never see.

I take thy innocence
From your eyes,
Into my palm,
Out through black fingers,
Onto a page.
I couldn't go on
Without taking thee.

I take thy belief,
Make it mine.
Your dribble
Becomes my flood,
A flood becomes
A book.
Without thee, nothing.

I take thy selflessness,
I take thy life,
I take thy soul.
Thou shalt know,
Thou impacted me.
I take thy interest,
I take thee."

Tears sting my eyes. I think I know what it means, but I don't say anything to him.

After a few minutes, he says, "Some people say their marriage vows like they can be undone. Did you ever think ours could really be undone?"

"Never," I whisper, "I've never been able to see beyond you."

"Why do you think I was working on my second PhD

when we met, yet I'd never written a single word of my own before you?"

I brush my cheek over his knee, again and again. It's times like this when nothing hurts anymore. I only want to expose myself to him, drown myself in him. I slide my hand over his meaty calf muscle and squeeze, relishing his body hair, his manliness… him.

"You are truly my missing rib, Ade. We make sense. Don't we?"

"We do."

"I can't breathe without you. I can't handle life without you. I don't know what I'm doing when I'm without you but I know, that with you, everything is better."

"You're older so you'll die first and then I'll die right after," I tell him, "because I couldn't imagine a life without you now. I'd die. I simply wouldn't live."

"Me too."

"I only lived for the kids when you died the first time. I was surviving on meagre rations of air and sustenance. I was alive only for them but I would have died if not for them and their needs. I remained alive for them. Without Billy, we wouldn't have even met. I would have let myself go so long ago, if it weren't for them. So you see, everything happens for a reason."

He turns my face so I have to look right at him. "Then you see why I have to do this film and why you have to be with me. It'll be rubbish without you. You're the soul of everything I do. I'm not warm or kind without you, Adrienne."

I see sadness in his eyes. "You're the most wonderful man I've ever known. Why do you doubt yourself?"

"Come here," he says, beckoning me.

I place our empty glasses on the side table and curl up on his lap. He holds me close as I stroke the soft edges of the gown he's wearing. Our noses touching, he bestows a little kiss on my lips.

"It's like when Frodo has to leave Middle Earth for the immortal lands. It's like that for me. It's like," he bites his lip, "they say time heals all but for me, there's a darkness inside me that I despise and I can't get rid of it, it's a hurt I cannot heal and it's who I am."

"I adore who you are, I want all of who you are. I love that. Let my light absorb your dark. I have always wanted it, always. I love you because I see you, and even when you don't think I see, I do. I see you."

I push my lips into his and kiss him, begging him to open his mouth, which he does. He opens for me and invites me in and our tongues roll and collide, the sweet heat of our drinks mingling, the tang of Irish whiskey bringing even hotter flames to my cheeks.

He pushes open my robe a little, exposing my right breast. Grasping me, he flicks my nipple and I wince.

"Have you expressed?"

"I did a bit in the bathroom, after you fucked me. They were leaking so bad."

He gives me those dark eyes, zeroing in, that venomous look. The beast stirs within, the one that lives inside him, the one he had to become to survive.

The animal once thrived, living off drugs and sex and easy days, but with one glance I somehow tamed him and made him want to be a better man. For some reason, I want to meet that animal he used to be. I feel dissatisfied knowing other women have known and witnessed the animal.

He leans down and pulls my nipple up to his mouth,

yanking on me.

I fall back slightly, my body hanging over the back of the armrest, bowing in submission.

He sucks hard and fluid leaves me, then he sucks harder for the rest and bites me hard too.

"I own this body. I don't think Daddy is good enough for you. I think you need a Master to make you see the errors of your ways."

"But I left the milk in a cup, in the bathroom–"

"Ah-ah-ah, no excuses for removing what is mine or David Junior's…"

He can be as vile as he wants to be tonight, I've always adored this dirty side of him. I have yearned for his ownership of me for so long.

Before I know it, he has his finger buried between my legs and his mouth is on my other breast, expressing more milk from me. He groans, like he really enjoys it, like he loves it even. Like it is the froth for his coffee, the elixir of his life, the whitener of his soul.

My robe is hanging off me now, my body exposed, the material slipping down from my shoulders so that when I stand it'll just fall right off.

He toys with my slit, moving moisture around, teasing me; flicking a nail over my clit, then pushing inside me, brushing against my g-spot, just enough to make my thighs clench. Heat builds and I reach a crescendo, my head thrown back, my hands hanging onto his neck.

"That's what I call a nice, slow-build orgasm. As you know Adrienne, I'm never content until I've made you cry out in fear."

It's always the fear that I'll never find pleasure so good again.

Yet it always remains so good, and in fact it just gets better.

Wobbly on my feet, he helps me stand and the robe falls somewhere. I couldn't care less about that now. I'm partially delirious from the heavy dinner tonight, the drink, the orgasms and now that strong Irish coffee.

I'm aware of where he's taking me but I'm already so relaxed, I just close my eyes and let him do what he wants. He places me on the bed, in the middle, all the covers pulled back.

"Davy will be drunk tomorrow… unless you feast in the morrow," I say, giggling like a naughty schoolgirl.

"You won't sleep at all tonight and when I'm done, you'll be bone-dry. I'll make sure of it. All the nastiness, I will draw from you, your pussy oozing its menace into me, your disgusting desires dragged kicking and screaming from you so you become pliant. You need the most thorough fucking of your life, don't you?"

"Yes," I gasp, "pretty please, Master."

"You want my cock, don't you?"

"Always."

"Fat and heavy inside you?"

"Always."

"Good."

My eyes are already shut but he puts his tie over me, blocking my vision, his strong hands knotting it beneath my head. He ties what feels like silk around my wrists and knots them together, then ties them to the head of the bed. It must be my silk scarf.

"Sorry but I'm going to have to improvise with your ankle holds."

"You're not sorry," I say cackling, "you degenerate."

"You better believe it."

"I do."

I hear him go to the bathroom and pick up my forgotten stockings, which he then uses to tie me to the bottom of the four-poster bed.

Naked and spread, I wonder what I look like to him. I don't have to ask, he begins to tell me…

"Your boobies will get smaller. I like them smaller, but I also like them full of milk. It's a toss-up for me."

"Oh yeah?"

"Umm-mmm." I hear his voice one side of the bed, then the other. He's circling his prey.

"Does this indulge your masterfulness?"

"It more than indulges, it encourages," he utters, still wandering the perimeter of the bed.

"I see. Well, as you can tell, I'm going nowhere. I'm right here for your delectation."

"And yet my delectation might need some considering. I have here a tasty body, awaiting examination. Infiltration, even."

"You make me sound like a military exploit."

He chuckles, revealing a mere soupçon of insecurity. "You've been without for so long Adrienne, I don't want to tear you up."

"I'll tell you when it hurts. Because hurt is different to pain, believe me."

"Hurt?" he asks, his voice coming from the foot of the bed where he no doubt stands, contemplating his next move. "Is it different to pain?"

"Much."

"Really?"

"And harm… that's a whole different ballgame."

"I see. So perhaps you would like to teach me?"

"Unless you want to grow a vagina and a uterus and try out childbirth, you'll never know the difference between pain and harm like a woman does. Believe me, a woman can wield pain like a sword if she's pushed. She can channel inner strength like no man on earth."

"Well, then… let me have a little think. It seems very clear to me, you need punishing in severe ways."

I grin. "Oh, Master…"

"Pain won't work for you, Adrienne. You need something much more sinister… torture… or me, toying with you."

I pout. "Please, Master. Tell me what you have in mind."

"Pleasure delay. Much… much… more pleasure delay than you can possibly imagine."

"Oh, no."

"When we get home, I'm going online to order some toys special delivery, so we can be in receipt of them as soon as possible. I have some nasty, disgusting little toys in mind to keep you in check. Tell me who gives you pleasure, little bunny."

"You do, Master."

Little bunny is the name he sometimes uses for me when I am sick or injured, like the time I fell off my horse and he nursed me constantly as my leg got better, calling me, "Little bunny, always thinking with her cunny."

That was another drought we tried to grin and bear our way through. With a broken leg, sex had been impossible. I got rid of the horse afterwards. I used to be mad on horses and then the thought of getting hurt and my children… I couldn't risk it. It was lucky because a few months after the horse fall, we were at it like rabbits and accidentally fell pregnant with David Junior. Anyway, I couldn't ride as I got bigger and bigger.

"Now bunny, are you ready?"

"What for?"

"You'll see…"

SIX

I'm still waiting here, exposed and anxious. What's he going to do with me? I have no idea. He's taking his time. I can't see and I can't escape. I'm completely naked and it's only been six months since I gave birth to my fourth child.

"Do you want to know about the first thing that attracted me to you?"

"Tell me," I whisper, as I wait for him to touch me.

"Your big eyes," he says, his quicksilver manner putting me on edge.

I know this man well but is there a darker side I have never met before? A version of him that could be pushed to actually harm me…

"My eyes?"

"I was in the library, reading in my corner as was my wont. I saw you walking through, on your way out probably. You bumped into your pal Bebe and the way your eyes lit up over a shared joke, it sliced a hole through my darkness, it stamped your seal on my heart. I knew I had to speak with you after that… and soon, as I saw you closer up, I realised who you were and I hated that you were already in my soul because I knew I would never be good enough for you. You were a better breed than me, always will be."

"David–"

"Shhh," he says, placing a finger over my lips. "I'm still not good enough for you but I don't think any man ever will be. The simple fact is, I know nobody will ever love you more than me. I knew it then, I know it now."

Two tears sprinkle the tie covering my eyes.

"I remember seeing you around Harrogate, when we were kids," he says, caressing the fallen tears as they soak through the tie and escape, "popular, surrounded by your friends. I never wanted you then. You weren't my sort of person, but then in another life, we met and you'd been forced to become my sort of person. The sort who'll do anything to survive."

"David–"

"No, Adrienne, listen. The porn stuff, I did it to survive. I am not ashamed of it but nor am I proud of it and nor did I really enjoy it. It was staged, it was fake… the women never orgasm and we took Viagra to stay hard all the time. When I think of it I feel sad because in fact, my body is yours and nobody else's. It should have always been yours."

I hate it when he talks like this; I can't take his sincerity, his deepness. The saying still waters run deep has never been more applicable for any other man.

"Listen to me when I say, I don't know why you still doubt yourself when all I see when I look at you is pure light, pure heaven. I could never not love you, Adrienne. You're perfect in so many ways, you don't even know."

With his hand, he caresses my side, catching the swell of my breast with a thumb, his warm palm travelling along cooling skin. I need his warmth. Shivering, I wriggle under his touch. His hand rests on my hip and he whispers, "The only thing I don't like about you is that you shut me out."

His words make my breath short, and I stop wondering about what pleasure he's going to give me, and start thinking about what he's going to try and get me to admit.

"It's your worst feature," he says, leaning down to kiss my navel, "but the rest of you… it's magical."

His kisses travel from my navel and coat the insides of my thighs. Immediately I'm warm again and I close my eyes even beneath the blindfold, desperate and willing him to pleasure me.

"Your pussy still tastes as beautiful as it ever did. Your skin is still as soft, your warmth still as hot, your legs as long as ever, your voice as arousing if not more now you're more mature, your lips still sumptuous, your tongue as wet, your beauty as alluring, your bum still as round and grabbable as ever, your breasts perfect, your neck long, your tiny button nose as cute, your chin adorable, your slight wrinkles indicative of wisdom, your thick hair so luxurious… and yet there's one major change in you that I can't put words to, nor describe."

"Please, David…"

"A deep part of me knows a deep part of you better than I did when we met and even though the man I am sees your beauty, the soul inside me sees more. He sees you've grown in kindness, in ability, in patience… in love. You have so much more love now than you ever did."

"Because of you, David. Because you're the chicken to my egg. Neither of us came before the other and yet without one another, we wouldn't exist. When I thought you dead, the essence of me was dead too. I feel exactly the same about you as you do for me. Love is time, David. Love is time and I want so much more time with you."

"Adrienne…"

He kisses my silky, bare mound, then leaves me unsatisfied, his kisses coming up from my navel again. He tugs a nipple gently on his way, then reaches my throat, rubbing his stubble against me, his kisses vociferous.

"Oh, David…"

He presses his lips to mine, letting me feel him, moving slowly into my mouth. So slowly and luxuriously, I want to push back, but I fear that he would be displeased if I did. I want to pull him fully on top of me but I can only feel him to the side, his erection at my hip, his rough pubes tickling my stomach. The smell of his cologne is spicy, and mixed with the musk of his juices, and the milky scent of his skin, the mix is potent because with my eyesight gone, my sense of smell is heightened. I want to explore every inch of him slowly, taste all the different scents he possesses. I want to pull at his hair, but I can't and this being tied-up thing is proving to be the most torturous punishment – and I cannot imagine anything else being so punishing, not yet anyway. I still wonder what is to come…

He licks slowly into my mouth, dragging sensations from me I can't separate. I'm boiling and simmering at the same time, seething and panting, moaning and groaning, and desperate for his cock inside me yet also desperate for the kiss to continue – for the luxury of it to never wane. The peace he gives me as he kisses me is wonderful and yet the lust it stirs inside me, maddening.

"David, Master, please…" I murmur against his lips.

"I warned you, Adrienne. I know how to pleasure you but that also means I know how to delay it. I know when you do come, it'll be much more satisfying for the delay."

"I can't see your face. I can't touch you… this is horrifying! I want to–"

I hear a ripping sound, the tearing of some sort of material, and then he's putting a gag around me. It's a bit of the napkin the hotel had wrapped around the champagne bucket to stop it dripping. I can taste wet metal on it.

In response I mumble words that make no sense, but hopefully he knows I mean, "It's not fair."

"Darling Adrienne, you wanted me in charge of you and now you have just that. In life you're so strong and so in charge but just occasionally, you need to have someone else pluck the strings."

How can he do this to me? Will I get a kiss now, or not?

Probably not now I'm gagged!

"The man in me, not the soul, is now going to tell you how much I love and lust after your body…"

I mumble incoherent words.

"You're so sweet, baby," he says, sounding almost innocent.

He's not!

"I love it when I catch sight of you in the shower and there's water dripping down your back, wetting the little blonde hairs all over your body. I love that those same hairs are currently stood on end. In fact even your bald pussy has risen gooseflesh…"

He strokes a fingertip over the baldness, and quick as a flash, digs his long finger deep inside me, then extracts it just as quick.

Panting, I can only see spots behind the blindfold. I would try to rub my thighs together but I'm tied up and spread.

“I love it whenever you bend over and the apple of your bottom protrudes in such a way, the sight draws heat straight into my cock.”

Oh my god. That is so hot. Him… getting hard… as I do my chores around the house.

“I love how you keep house like a sergeant major, it drives me insane,” he admits, “seeing you scrubbing, your waist going side to side, those scruffy jeans you wear hanging off the edge of your hips, skin exposed between the waistband and your t-shirt… and don’t get me started on the way you look as you feed our boy with all that flesh of yours on show. I sometimes want to throw you down to the ground right away and suck on you myself.”

I mumble, desperate for touch… for something.

I hear him move to the suitcase, unzipping it.

“I came prepared,” he says.

Oh god, what is he going to do?

I hear the squeeze of liquid and a low chuckle from him.

“Relax,” he warns me, then he pokes at my anus.

It’s cold I feel, cold wetness.

I try to level my breathing, taking in deep, long breaths, and before long my nerves around my sphincter are tingling and he finds a path inside.

My sex drive is on fire and I want to fuck his finger, and I want to come from anal penetration, but as we’ve found in the past it’s difficult for me to come from that alone. David finds it much easier to enjoy anal orgasms, his prostate so easy to find, his sex drive higher than mine.

I still enjoy it as he pushes inside, pushing and pushing.

“Your arse smells of bouillabaisse,” he says, and I feel a little disgusted.

But I can’t think long on that as he methodically teases

me, slipping in and out of me, building a pace and a rhythm. It's a pleasure/pain thing that is hard to remember afterwards, but for some reason I always want to try it again.

He squeezes more lube from the bottle and adds another finger to my hole, fucking me with two fingers.

"I can't tell you how hot it is, watching you like this. Your big, fat, milky tits are pointing to the sky even though they're so full. Your nipples could cut glass by the look of them."

With prickly heat spreading around my skin, I wish I could demand that he fuck me now and have done.

"Do you want to know the naughtiest thing you do without realising it?" he asks. "And let me tell you, you do it all the time, so it's no wonder I'm hard all the fucking time."

I nod as best I can.

"You forget to wash sometimes, no doubt too busy to remember to wash, and the smell of you gets more… pungent… and it makes me fucking rampant for you, you hot, dirty slut," he says, pushing more eagerly into my dark depths, my tight anus, and a third finger is added.

I want to scream, "Noooooooooo!!!"

There's more adding of lube, too.

"Then," he says with a chuckle, "there's the mornings I wake up with you pushed up against my hard cock and I don't know whether to ravage you or make you suck it."

Ravage me!!!!!

"But I'm too gentleman for that."

Sweat beads on my forehead. He's almost all the way in.

It's so tight down there, I feel like I might pass out. I can feel how thin the barrier is between my vagina and other channel. I can feel how tight and crushed everything seems.

I've loosened and relaxed and now he's squeezing more

from the bottle.

"Relax," he says, and I know he's spreading me even wider.

There's a moment of stasis, of nothing, and even though I know what is happening, it feels as though it's not happening to me.

He's got his whole fist in now, thumb and all.

He doesn't move because we both know if he does, I could tear.

He slowly flexes his fingers, in and out, in and out, stretching and then closing. The most amazing thing happens. I suck him right in. Then I feel as though I'm close to climax.

Please don't stop it... don't delay it... please.

I nod my head fast, throw my head back and lift my hips.

He keeps going.

"I've wanted to try this for a long time..."

He keeps going with the motion, not thrusting, just stretching me then letting me relax. Fingers spreading and then collapsing again. Flexing with just enough power to let me know he's buried in the innermost part of me.

I dig my heels in the bed as the tightness sends me into a tailspin that's unstoppable now. It's a much different kind of orgasm, no less intense, but different. When I come, I feel myself bearing down on him hard and more of my inner muscles burn with the sensation of growing tightness and contractions that I'm completely not in control of, not at all.

Gently, he removes himself and I somewhat space out as I listen to him walk slowly to the bathroom, where he thoroughly washes his hands.

"Tell me I'm the only one to ever do that," he demands, and I nod, because it's true. I've had anal sex with others but nothing ever as good as that, nothing ever as sexual and intimate. It's the trust between us.

"I want you so much, Adrienne. Do you want to feel how much I want you?"

YES!!!

But somehow I know he's still intent on punishing me – prolonging my real pleasure – that of having him really make love to me.

"Here," he says, and he straddles my shoulders, putting himself in my mouth.

He's hot and his skin feels tough under the weight of his arousal. I can barely fit him between my lips. When he's like this, I sometimes fear he won't fit – he won't be satisfied easily.

He withdraws and shame rushes down my spine, like red-hot heat.

"I need you so much," he says, "so very much."

He shifts on the bed, but I'm not sure of where he's going, nor what his plan is.

"Baby… girl… my bunny and her very hot cunny…"

Fuck me already!

I want his body on top of mine, his cock digging deep inside me, his arms around me, my hands in his hair, our breaths mingling, mouths non-concentric, my hands able to feel him, touch him, provoke him. Like this, I can do nothing at all.

He presses the very large but rounded top of the lube bottle to my vagina and with a pop, it enters me. As wet and as aroused as I am, I take it, even though it's hard and unyielding unlike a real dick.

He starts fucking me with it and it's painful but enticing, making me move my hips onto it every time he brings it deeper into me.

"More lube, Adrienne?"

More cock, more like!

"No? Okay then…"

He sits between my spread legs and fucks me with the bottle, then leans down to lick my clit.

I experience that terrifying moment when I fear he will take away his tongue, thus removing the glorious sensation of his soft touch, which electrifies my every nerve ending every time he flicks the tip of his muscle against my tiny knot of exquisite nerves.

I mumble words again, trying to tell him how desperately I love him, and our connection must enable him to know what I'm saying because he replies, "I love you, too."

Then he damn well takes his tongue away.

Not the tongue!

Of all the delights he possesses, giving me his tongue and then taking it away is surely the cruellest trick he could exact on me.

Shaking my head side to side, he chuckles loudly and keeps screwing me with the lube bottle.

"I don't know if I've ever been so hard, Adrienne. I've fucked so many women but the sight of my one true lady love… like this… it's not just the stuff of fantasies, it's the stuff of mind-altering euphoria."

I mumble frantically, words not decipherable this time.

"I sometimes pump my hand up and down my cock in the shower, to fantasies of you, sat naked on your goddess throne, except for a garland about your hair, the sun shining down on you, displaying all of you to everyone. Mostly in the fantasies, I see half a dozen women touching and preening you, preparing you for me. They paint your body, tuck your breasts into tight clothes and rub cream all over your legs and feet. They also kiss you, suck your breasts, lick your cunt until you're ready for me, and then I imagine myself waiting in bed. I'm already hard and all you do is slide straight onto me, slide so swift and deep, then ride me like the goddess you are, until dragging cum from me into your belly. I imagine the girls watching all the while as they watch their goddess own her prince, own him like nobody else can, and then I imagine your minions taking you to the bath, cleaning me out of you until you're pure again. Then they lick and suck you all night, all of them, because I'm wasted and spent and they can collectively feed your needs all night long."

My hips rise off the bed, my body flailing as much as it possibly can, in rebellion. In protest. It felt like I was right there in his fantasy and now my desperation is palpable.

"Time to come," he says, his words an instruction.

My facial expression must be ugly, because it's like I'm being electrocuted. I'm squeezing so hard at the unyielding object between my legs, and I'm drenching the bed beneath me. Orgasming against my own will. I want to come with him, not for him.

I loll, absolutely drained.

How could he do this to me?

SEVEN

I come to, not sure what just happened then. I'm not sure where I am either or what I'm feeling. Maybe overwhelmed. Maybe a little disgusted. A little out of sorts.

Awareness dawns on me. I'm untied and in his arms. I feel numb. I'm almost asleep.

But I'm free and back in his arms.

"Hmm," he moans, his bristles at the back of my neck, his arms cupping my body.

We're spooning.

I reach my arm behind me, grasping his hair.

He licks my throat and pinches my breast, prompting me to pull harder on his hair.

"You're so cruel," I accuse, and he replies, "I know."

His laughter breaks before mine but we end up laughing together.

When his hand trails down, caressing my stomach, the atmosphere changes and his breathing ups, becomes heavier, hoarser. I let my hand wander and feel his erection, still full and by now, no doubt frantic.

"I'm so tired," I pretend, trying to punish him like he

punished me.

"I'll fuck you as you sleep, it doesn't bother me."

"I thought you said you were a gentleman."

"It's okay milady, I know I'm just your bit of rough."

"And very nice you are for my bit of rough."

We begin grinding against one another, the dance recommencing.

His cock slots between my ample bum cheeks and he's mimicking fucking me, his hands shaking as he grasps my boob, then flesh, then my boob again.

I remember I've missed his kisses and I turn my head.

His mouth's on me at once, pressing and seeking, tongue with no finesse. Straight in there. He's losing patience now, I can tell. He's laboured for so long to ensure my pleasure and now he's at breaking point, wanting his own.

I roll over and on top. My enjoyment is immense as his hands stroke up and down the back of me, grabbing and tugging. I want to slide straight down onto him.

I'm nipping his mouth when he pushes me up so we're sat facing one another.

I'm almost pulsating as I look at him, so handsome and eager, straining to contain himself.

"Haven't you got what you wanted?" I whisper. "You could have used me at any point."

"I'd rather have consent, always."

I mess his hair up. His hands are on my shoulders, stressing my skin, his need immense, his cheeks stained with hot lust.

I grab the errant bottle of lube and stroke a large amount of it up and down his lovely big penis.

Grabbing and tugging, I reach under and put pressure on his perineum and within moments, he's coming in my hand, his desire erupting into my grasp for the second time in a night.

We remain seated, his eyes closed, his desire sated for now. I put my hands on his shoulders, ejaculation mingling with sweat. We'll sleep in it all tonight and we'll revel in it until we have to wash it all away in the morning.

I kiss his cheeks and his shut lids, his ears and his eyebrows and hair.

"You're still too gentle with me," I complain.

"I could never hurt you, Adrienne," he whispers, "not even pretend. I couldn't possibly ever do it. You're too precious to me."

"But what if I demanded it from you?"

His eyes shoot open and he searches mine in the dim light of the room, lit only by one table lamp in the distance and the light of the fire.

"You can't demand anything from me, I say what happens to you in the bedroom."

I pout. "What if I wanted just a little bit of spanking? On my bottom."

He presses his lips together. "Just a bit?"

I move closer to cuddle him, wrapping him tighter in my arms. "Just a little."

He smoothes a hand over my rump. "Here?"

"Yes, there."

He smashes his large, firm hand against me, making me buck towards him. It stings in the aftermath and he sucks my shoulder, asking again, "You really want it?"

"Hmm-mmm."

"Then you have to earn it. Get sucking."

I sneak down to my front and suck him into my mouth, able to draw him in deep, in his semi-hard state.

Soon he's so big I can only take in the head.

"Enough. Good girl."

He drags me closer, laying me across his lap, butt-up.

"You want me to tan this?"

"PLEASE."

He thrashes me.

"Thank you, Master."

"Again?"

"I'll tell you when to stop."

He takes my other cheek, stinging that side too. He keeps going and the crack of his hand against me makes my vagina weep with pleasure. I've always liked rough, angry sex with him but it's difficult to get him to snap. He's so controlled.

"Are you done? You're beetroot now."

I pant fast. "I don't know, am I done?"

I've lost count of his strikes, immersed in the blank space of coping with pain, my mind elsewhere and unconcerned with anything.

"You're done."

He throws me on my back and I spread my legs for him. My head's not on a pillow. I don't know which way up the bed I am. I just want him on top of me, pushing me down, forcing me into the mattress. I watch as he quickly rolls on a condom.

He jumps on top and slides deep into me, balls deep, my body giving him a welcome home.

The way his muscles roll under my touch makes me more excited as I watch his eyes focus on my mouth, on my breasts shifting with his thrusts. He's moving fast, not careful.

"Yes," I goad, clinging to him, "yes."

As he pushes me down, I feel the stinging, burning backs

of my buttocks roll into the cool sheets, the motion a repeated reminder of his strength and my trust, and also my desire for adrenalin… for more… for passion.

He leans into me, kissing me harshly, ripping out my tongue towards his.

"Yes, yes," I repeat.

He drags me up off the bed, pulling us to sitting again.

I wrap my legs around him and he buries himself in my neck, vicious groans escaping his mouth.

He's had his pleasure already but this is different. This is war against the forces that have tried to pull us apart. This is pleasure beyond pleasure, this is us taking tonight and making it something to remember, something to think about when life gets busy again after the holidays.

I wrap my arms behind his head and cling to his hair, tugging and fisting it, crying out with pleasure, over and over. We've got a delicious rhythm going and the bed's creaking but it doesn't matter. We're making noises but I don't care if anyone hears or knows.

"I love you," I groan, tossing my head back.

He leans back a little on one arm, his body holding almost all my weight, and the leverage sends him deeper into me and the hallowed A-spot buried deep inside me begins to churn my muscles inside out and I don't know what's happening…

Minutes, or it could be hours, pass by as I tumult on the hardness my husband possesses, as I crescendo and plummet over and over, but not quite… not quite reaching the peak.

I dig my hands in his shoulders and demand, "Just ravish me!"

I'm flipped over and he uses me like a wheelbarrow, legs up, his cock shoving into me as I'm pulled half-off the bed, my elbows digging into the mattress to steady myself.

"Your arse looks fucking amazing!" he yells.

"Oh god, oh god… oh fuck!!" I scream as he fills me so deep, so deep, so very deep, a rush of pleasure striking me, the sensation of boneless, weightless heat hitting me first in my thighs and hips, then down to my knees, back up and everywhere. It's so exquisite, it draws me down and under, then back up again for air. I almost don't want this to happen. My clit is burning!

I'm climbing to an impossible precipice, somewhere unreachable, and I scream his name as he pummels my clit and makes me come all over again.

I collapse into the bed, absolutely bereft, totally without shame, without pain or injury or harm.

He falls on top of me, growling into my ear, "That felt so fucking amazing. God you make my cock hard. You make me unhinged."

Biting my shoulder, he scoops and rolls me, pulling me into his hold once more, spooning from behind.

We recover slightly and catch our breaths. Then he pulls me onto his chest, my face buried between his arms and pecs.

I kiss his nipple and mewl, stroking a hand up and down his body, pulling the condom off him and throwing it onto a discarded towel.

He kisses my forehead. "I love how your pussy farts when you come that hard."

I giggle. "You're a sicko. I heard nothing."

"That's because you were screaming. I was back there, listening."

We laugh again.

He pulls the covers over us and slowly we begin to fall

asleep, completely absorbed by each other, nothing bothering, nothing broken.

"I'm going to eat breakfast off your stomach in the morning. I'm going to suck honey from your tits. I hope this is okay."

"I'm going to let you, I hope this is okay? You won't think less of me…" I say, stroking his spent willy as we lay, cuddling.

He pulls my lips to his and kisses me very gently, barely capturing me, just a little light pressure on my bottom lip.

"I had my hand buried deep in your arse tonight. I hardly think anything you do could make me think less of you."

I squeeze my eyes shut, slightly embarrassed as I sober up and think back to it. Giggling behind my hand, I tell him, "Shut up, you've had my hand up yours."

"Yes and I hadn't just eaten a six-course meal… the things I do…"

I grimace. "You're spoiling what was a lovely night."

He nips my top lip between his teeth. "I loved all of it, I hope you did."

I squeeze his shoulders. "I want to be your little toy. I like it very much indeed. I want nastier things… if we can get any nastier. What do you think?"

He snarls, "I can get much, much nastier. I have tortures galore planned for you. We'll just have to get a very good lock on the door at home."

I snicker into his armpit. "Oh god, yes!"

The frivolity passes as we lay quiet and after a while, I kiss his mouth quietly, gently, just little pecks. He lies there, watching me, letting me have my way. He's almost staring blankly, perhaps fascinated really, or maybe he's too moved to show it.

I wrap myself around him so tight as I drift off, but before I do, I whisper, "I am so deeply in love with you, I'm lighter than a feather, drunker than a sailor on leave, happier than a girl in new boots, but more importantly, more at peace than I ever thought possible."

David doesn't do crying but when he looks at me with a frown, I know I've touched his heart.

"Go to sleep bunny, your brave little heart needs the rest. You made me proud tonight. I am so proud when you let me take care of you."

"I love you so much," I repeat, burying myself as deep into his chest as I can get, "I don't think I could love you another ounce more. I'm full up with love."

Then as I'm almost asleep, I hear a couple of sniffs and watch as he uses his free hand to wipe some of his tiny tears away.

I sometimes have to remind myself David isn't as strong as me. It's a secret I keep to myself.

He tries to be but he isn't, not really. I used to think he was stronger, but he was always just trying to be strong for my sake. He has never had my will to thrive. I expect that will contributed to my eventual downfall, but it also forced me to climb back out of the cavernous desolation I found myself in, too. I've come to see over time, I have strength I've yet to mine, hidden depths yet to explore. I'm still discovering myself, all the time. David's very simple in comparison. Some days he doesn't write which is fine. He can go without. He wants love and a family more than anything, whereas I want to make a stamp on the world. I am always thinking about how I can better the world. I give hugely to charity through my business on the side and show my face at lots of events. Dad tells me about new investments and some I do invest in, others I don't, but I always enjoy the pursuit – the research of a new venture. It's only David who tries to slow me down. It's only he who reminds me I'm just one woman. Somehow, we work.

I sometimes sit and think, *he simply wouldn't have survived what I have.*

In a way though, his comparative innocence is what keeps me sane.

Hopefully he will never know what it is to kill a man, nor break a man… nor will he ever find out what it's like to see your partner die before you do. I endured all these things.

I want him to one day see that me giving myself up to him is proof of my strength and my willingness to love. By submitting my mind to him, even just for a little while, that gives me peace the like of which I'm not sure he will ever comprehend. For a woman to trust a man and submit wholly to him, it's the only true piece of calm a woman ever experiences as he fills that hole inside, a hole not literal but metaphorical, a desperate yearning we have for one simple thing – escape.

For the weight of the world sometimes rests on our shoulders.

EIGHT

Christmas Eve

Last night I thought he was joking but I'm tied to the bed again and he's actually eating breakfast off my stomach. I haven't even washed yet!

"Stop it!" I giggle because I'm embarrassed and he's tickling me.

I have a pile of pancakes and syrup all over my midriff and he's carving his breakfast right on top of my skin. Granted he's being careful not to cut me, though he couldn't, not with that blunt-ish knife, but he's bloody well treading dangerously nonetheless.

"Yummm, hmmmm, mmmmm," he says, his eyes big and greedy.

I laugh, I can't help but laugh.

I guess at least I'm not gagged this time, nor blindfolded. Just tied to four corners of the bed, unable to stop my naked husband feasting off my body.

"It's so sticky!" I complain.

Mischievous David is in the house and he winks, "I know!"

Earlier on, he opened the hotel room door wearing his robe and I was already tied to the bed. He insisted he be allowed to take the tray straight away otherwise the room service waiter would have got more than a little surprise to see me spread, naked.

David's got me on a bed of pillows to raise me off the bed slightly so he doesn't have to lean over so much but I can still feel syrup leaking over my sides and onto the pillows! Someone will have a great clear-up operation on their hands after we leave later on. I dread to think it, but I expect someone will be staying in this room throughout the Christmas break, what with this hotel offering packages that last the entire season. I mentally make an apology to them and the service people who will make up this room after we're gone.

Over on the little dining table by the window I can see my own breakfast beneath a hood, waiting for me. David's offered me some of his but I've rebelliously declined because all I want is my bacon and eggs beneath that hood!

"Almost finished," he says, and I giggle, because he's cutting gently again and tickling me.

"I'll get you back for this, Lewis."

"Maybe… we'll see." Rubbing his belly in circles, he groans, satisfied. "Pancake à la Adrienne, it tasted good."

"Now please untie me?"

The damn man puts his used cutlery on the bedside table and lays himself between my open legs. He's just been sat between them, reaching over my pussy for his food, but now he's laid between them it feels all the more naughty.

In daylight I can see the brown of his eyes so much better and he's searching my eyes too. His arms and hands wrapped beneath me, I'm powerless to fend him off.

He lets me taste the syrup on his lips as he gives me a chaste kiss, the bristles of his growing stubble scrubbing at my sensitive skin.

"David," I moan as he kisses along my throat, a mixture of feathery kisses, then lush kisses, tender kisses and sloppy kisses.

I wish I could lock my ankles together but I'm tied up.

Oh but I am a stupid woman! It's only stockings holding me down.

I yank at my holds and the silk frays, then eventually gives. Soon I'm able to lock my feet together between his back and his response is to take a morning draught from my breast.

"I wish I could pump my cum deep into your belly," he growls.

"Well you could but it would still be a risk, even with breastfeeding…"

"But you haven't had a period…"

"It's still a risk! Your potency is dangerous, darling. We need you tied up and quickly. I fear just looking at you might make me pregnant sometimes. Just one look and… if I didn't know the pain of childbirth, I'd lay right down and let you do the nasty without thought if I couldn't remember the pain… and the responsibility that comes after."

"Fuck, but I want it…"

"I know," I groan in response, as he slips down and pushes his tongue between my folds.

"Ah god, ah… ah…"

He strokes me to breaking point, sucks me until I'm on the edge, and then thankfully he puts on a condom and pushes inside me, just as I'm so close to coming. The intrusion is shocking and breaks my ability to focus and follow through, halting my pleasure. He lets my hands free but keeps them above my head with his hands through mine.

"Let's make love," he says, and I smile, an almost-innocent smile.

"Your wish is my command–"

He buries himself deep, his teeth at my shoulder, and I almost tell him to get off my shoulder because he's bitten it enough already while we've been in this hotel room.

I'm also very sore down below and kind of glad for the condom!

I'm also aware of the fact that my body knows it's been thoroughly fucked and will rebel against me later when my legs go stiff and my back needs rubbing from the excess pleasure. I'll need a deep Epsom salts bath and I'll need it without interruption from kids who might spot marks on me, or a husband wishing to cause me more grief!

I giggle in his ear and he asks, "What's going on in that head of yours?"

I try to control myself. "I was just thinking that when we get home I'll be walking like I've been riding three days straight."

"Haven't you?" He chuckles loudly, thrilling me.

I wrap my arms around his back and stare into his eyes as he carefully pushes his hips into mine, his legs working hard, his arms holding him up beneath me.

I dig my feet into the already destroyed mattress and lever, meeting him thrust for thrust, helping him find all those little pressure points inside me which are so sensitive and don't need much encouragement.

It becomes so that we're not two, but one, everything locked and joined so neatly we can move at will, our rhythm so tight we know how far we can go before he falls out. His strokes become long and I make sure his cock connects with my clit and slides along my upper wall.

I'm in a sweat within minutes and holding his cheeks, keeping his eyes. I'm soaking him and myself. He likes looking down to where we're joined and also growls every time he sucks my lactating nipples. He's nasty when he wants to be.

"Harder… faster," I ask, because I need this to get freaky. I need him so much.

As he picks up speed, I let him push me hard into the mattress and I hold onto his arms, feeling them lock, solid, working tirelessly. I don't suppose he needs to do his morning workout, not today!

"Oh god," I moan, approaching the point of no return, when no matter what he does I will come anyway.

He slows for some reason and looks down into my eyes, demanding I look right at him, smoothing hair out of my eyesight and off my forehead. He dips his tongue against mine and curls around me, lavishing me with his ardour. He's slowed and the long strokes have abated but I still feel my orgasm about to peak, about to scream its way out of me.

He pulls out and I almost cry, begging for mercy.

He removes the condom.

I'm scared but he hushes me.

"I need to feel you," he says, and he rubs his cock against my clit.

"I could still–"

"I won't do that," he murmurs against my wet lips, kissing me.

"I love you, David, please!" I cry, clinging onto him.

"Hush, just trust me," he whispers, and I stare, dumbfounded, wondering what he's going to do.

I'm anxious, ready, and spaced out. I need to come already. I'm pulsing, needing him quick, just sharp and fast. *Just do me already!* I want to scream.

"Just once," he murmurs, and he pushes balls deep into me, sheathless and naked, hot and beautiful.

A couple of thrusts and my eyes are squeezed tight shut, my body's bearing down on him, and that soda stream effect of everything bubbling and fizzing and drawing him back makes me almost pass out – the wait for it all having been unbearable.

He yanks me up quickly and stuffs himself into my mouth.

I taste lust and desperation and I hear the animal release, his cries of joy untamed, unleashed. I revel in him wanting to use me, and abuse me, sexually – just like this.

He forces his massive cock deep enough I want to be sick and I swallow my guts and breathe fast through my nose. He pulls my hair and I catch sight of him in ecstasy, his control gone, his body given up to me as he shuts his eyes and throws his head back. I dig my nails deep into his solid buttocks and scratch with all the venom I have. This is my bastard and I can use him, too.

A huge, gigantic load of cum falls down the back of my throat and I wince from the sharp, red-hot pain of it all.

I'm coughing as I pull away and he's too tired to comfort me right away. He falls to his knees on the bed, his head hanging loose.

"Go and have breakfast now, Adrienne. And you better sit there naked. I'll start the shower."

There's no cuddling and I'm upset.

He shuffles off without looking at me and I feel ashamed.

I thought I just gave him the most wonderful pleasure? It

sure felt like he was enjoying himself.

I pass by the windows naked, some of the curtains drawn, some open.

I see people up and about, walking the grounds already. It's unlikely they'll spot me like this, up on the third floor, but they could. There's always a chance they might spot me.

I sit and enjoy my breakfast and find the coffee in the pot still warm as well.

I'm probably soiling the upholstered chair but I don't really care.

"Ready when you are," he says, popping his head around the door and then shutting himself inside the bathroom.

I finish my eggs and bacon, then stand by the window, looking down on the world with my arms folded. I get lost staring at the topiary and the dead shrubs, dormant for winter, when I realise an elderly couple are whispering things behind their hands, like they've just seen me. They quickly dash behind a hedge, never to be seen again probably, and I wonder if they did see anything! I only hope it was nobody we know – I doubt it was. Most people from the party last night would have gone straight home or stayed at a cheap hotel, not the luxury one we're at. We never skimp on rare breaks like this. The limo was an expense too because this hotel is miles from the venue last night, but anyway…

"Come on, Ade!" he yells, and I realise I'm not very content with him stuffing himself inside my mouth and then just treating me like a whore, basically.

I stride to the bathroom and shut the door behind me. I can barely see for the steam.

"Get in here," he demands, and I enter the cubicle, shutting another door on the bed and the scene I was just a part of.

He grabs me in his arms from behind, his body covering mine in warmth and strength, and I ask, "Do you think what we just did was disgusting?"

"No I think it was beautiful and it shocked me how much more deeply I feel about you, every time we have a morning like this. Your body is such a delicacy, to me anyway. I'm so absorbed by you that sometimes, it still scares me."

I turn and face him. "Hold me and kiss me."

He holds me and kisses me under the rainfall shower for a very long time, smiling in between kisses, bruising my mouth even more than it already is.

"I think an old couple saw me naked. I think they might be behind some topiary now, speaking about or doing unsightly things… or maybe that's just my imagination."

"Never knock imagination, sweetheart."

We laugh and after the laughter dies down, he washes my hair and tenderly cleans my sore sex. He kisses my legs, up and down, and rubs lotion all over my body once we're out of the shower.

"I've loved this," I murmur as we dress in the room, getting ready to leave.

"So have I, more than I can say. I missed you so much, you know? It felt like my son stole you for a bit."

"He did," I confess, "like only a son of yours could."

My stomach roils at the thought of how much I miss my kids when we go away like this. The guilt is sometimes unbearable but it has got easier over the years. We'll go back to them today refreshed and less sex-deprived, for sure. I do wonder if Rachel's been okay, though. Did she have to get up and feed David Junior in the night or did he sleep through again? Did Marissa and Lucinda play nicely or were they fighting cat and dog, still? Did Billy try and sneak his boyfriend in again or is Rachel as wise to that as I am? I'm looking forward to a house full on Christmas day when my dad brings his new girlfriend Julie. There will also be Rachel's husband, the luscious Egyptian, Dr Kers who will tell the kids stories of mystery and intrigue over hot cups of cocoa, late on Christmas night.

"I love everything we have together," I tell David as we finish packing.

"Me too, little bunny."

Checking all the unsightly messes are buried beneath towels or sheets, we leave the room and head downstairs.

*

In the reception hall as we check out, I can't believe it but I spot the girl from last night. A part of me is fuming, while another part of me can't help but judge this as comical farce. Unless she's stalking him…

After David's paid the bill, he turns and spots the girl, who is seated in the sitting area, pretending to read.

When she lifts the book she's reading closer to her face, giggling to herself, we see it's one of David's.

She turns and realises we're leaving, then she leaps off her seat.

"Excuse me, excuse me!" she says as we attempt to leave before she embarrasses herself. "Will you sign my book?"

He looks at me and we look at the book together, trying to see which one it is. It's the first crime novel he had published.

David sighs. "Who's it to?"

"Me! Me, of course. Bernadette, you can call me Bernie though. Or Bee. Whatever." She sounds extremely nervous.

"Why did you leave dinner?" I ask.

"I wasn't well… it was the fish, I think. I mean… I can't be sure, but I should have known better. I was all set to enjoy my luxury stay here as well and now it's been ruined… still, at least I'm getting a signature off my favourite author."

David finishes signing the book and hands it to her. She checks the inscription and reads, "'To Bernie, or Bee, or Whatever. You have a nice smile. Love, David.'"

"Oh…" she murmurs, slightly disappointed or taken aback, I can't tell.

"I'm off, I don't know about you," he says, and he turns swiftly and leaves the reception hall, taking our luggage with him to the Jag.

"He's charming, isn't he?" I try to console her.

"He's as dry in real life, then? I'm surprised."

"I'm sorry, but… you're a fan of his novels? You don't–"

"Oh yes, I've been reading them since the beginning. He's really good."

I narrow my eyes. "But you… did you know he's been in film, too?"

"No… what film? Can I buy it?"

"It was just a student thing," I quickly say, finding a cover, "I don't think it's available. Maybe in a couple of people's lofts somewhere, but that's it…"

I get to thinking about Kat. Has she stitched us up, or something?

I am going to wring her throat…

"Tell him I said thanks and it was lovely to meet him. He really is as dry as the protagonist of his novels?"

"Drier," I remark.

"Amazing," she says, still staring at the inscription he wrote down for her. "Thanks again. I'm really sorry I never spoke last night but I was sort of star struck. It happened when I queued for Stephen King, you know! I was almost sick on him."

"So… you work with Kat?" I ask, wanting the nitty gritty.

She's staring at the book, absentmindedly aware of me still being here. "Yeah, I'm new. Kat's screwing Mika, did you know?"

She lifts her head, staring me straight in the eye. "And that baby his wife's carrying, it's not his you know. She's been seeing a man two doors down from her."

"How do you know–"

"I just know," responds Bernie, or Whatever Her Name.

"I wonder what will happen then…" I think out loud.

Bernie, who seems to have wisdom beyond her young years, looks straight in my eye. "Oh Kat won't have him back. She tells us that he's good in the sack but shit at life stuff. Like being there when it counts, you know? She says he's good at all the dirty stuff… but absolutely useless in a panic. Like the time she lost her brother and he reacted by sending her to Kos for three weeks, where she got a taste for young men…"

"Wow, you should perhaps be a writer yourself, Bernie."

"Maybe… or maybe I'll let the likes of David whisk me away into other worlds, drier worlds, more real worlds even."

"Goodbye, then," I say, excusing myself quickly.

She seems to barely notice me leave.

I jump in the car and David screeches off fast.

"What if people link the author version of me with the porn version? It's so far remained a secret, but what if–"

I cut him off. "You were had by Kat. I just asked that girl

if she'd ever seen you in film and her response was one of puzzlement. She was shy last night because you're an author she loves and she was star struck."

"Then why did Kat–" He shakes his head, already knowing the answer. "She saw me in a film. Now it makes sense. Kat's older and probably has a copy in her library. I bet she has a fucking library."

"I doubt she'll be bragging about having a library though! Anyway that Bernie girl just told me what everyone seems to know… that her and Mika are still shagging. In fact she also told me that Mrs Pietersen the second is sprogged up with a man from down the road's kid, not Mika's…"

"You couldn't make that shit up!" he laughs as we head for the motorway.

"Still, I can't help feeling that Kat did us a little bit of a favour… maybe."

"Maybe she did but if I have anything to do with it, she'll never step foot inside our house again! I'm not having the kids find out…"

"Oh god, who cares? I know loads of people whose parents were adult movie makers. So what?"

He growls. "Don't test me on this one thing. It's my choice and they are not to know!"

"Okay, okay," I say gently, trying to level the atmosphere which has suddenly become so tense.

With his one hand on the wheel and the other on his thigh, I take that hand and squeeze it. He squeezes back and tucks my hand under his thigh, where I usually have my hand when we're driving alone together.

I sit with my thoughts, sensing David needs his too.

I just wonder if perhaps myself and Kat are very alike, both strong women, needful of a man who can take charge not just in the bedroom but in life too. I guess it's hard to find the whole package when you're as strong as what we are. Because she and I are pretty strong characters, and even though it's not her best move going back there with Mika, I fully understand how that one man gets under your skin and never gets out. I feel like that with David. I'm just glad David is better with the life stuff. He tries, anyway.

A thought occurs to me as we hit the motorway and pick up speed. Once we're cruising, I tell him, "I'd rather have the real man than the author or the porn star any day, because the real man is imperfect and that's why I love him so much."

He grins slightly, looking sideways for a moment.

"I don't like that Kat," he argues, "she scares me. I'm all for strong women but she seems out of control."

"Love can do that to a person."

"What? You think she actually loves him?"

"I think it's more than love, what she and Mika have. I think it's their souls knowing they have that thing, you know… soul compatibility, but for them I don't think what they have fits in with real life. Maybe we should count ourselves lucky everyday we have that thing going on at the same time as managing real life too."

"Just you breathing makes me feel lucky," he retorts, and I wonder if I shouldn't finally read one of his books. When he is being his true self he is very dry; it's one of the many things I love about him.

NINE

Christmas Day

Yesterday when we got home it was madness and chaos, all the kids bouncing around, excited for Christmas – for presents and chocolates and the prospect of Granddad coming to stay. All my kids love my father. It's still very difficult between us two but it's getting easier all the time.

We got through the door and didn't have time to breathe!

Now it's Christmas morning, me and Rachel are creeping downstairs. It's six and we're making a start on prep. We also need to get the turkey in. Once we're in the safe confines of the kitchen, she gives me a big hug and whispers, "A very merry Christmas, sweetheart."

"You, too."

We begin dragging stuff from the fridge while also setting things going for breakfast, like coffee and freshly squeezed orange, a special treat reserved only for this day of the year. And maybe New Year's too. We have a lovely big kitchen with airy high ceilings and large appliances, plus an under-heated floor and a big range which heats up the room almost the minute you put it on. I'm thankful for it this morning, what with a deep frost outside.

"How were the kids while we were away? I never got chance to ask you yesterday! I got Davy thrust into my arms and then you had to go and finish off your Christmas shopping."

She had rushed off, like she was in a hurry to get away as quickly as possible.

"I had a barney with Billy if truth be told and I didn't want it to escalate so I just left…"

I turn and look at her. "He didn't?"

She grimaces. "Afraid so."

"Well I'll have to get David to talk with him today, as soon as possible. I'm not having this anymore. This is our house, our rules."

"I told him the same. I was just… he gave me the worst backchat yet. I couldn't… I couldn't get through to him."

I hear the sorrow and the conflict within her voice. Billy's fifteen and since he came out a couple of years ago, he's been flaunting the rules, like we'll go easy on him just because he's gay.

That's at least three times now that one of us has found him fooling around with his boyfriend in his bedroom, when we said that sort of thing isn't allowed under our roof, at least not until he's sixteen.

"You know I thought all those years he hated me was because of me and David splitting up and everything else but I can't help but worry sometimes that he inherited his father's temperament. I just can't help it, Rachel."

She rushes over, hearing the emotion in my voice. "It's understandable. God, I would fear the same thing. In fact he doesn't have any of the same mannerisms as you. He's definitely his father's child."

Marcus, the man who beat me up, fathered Billy and my firstborn has always been a handful. David seems to be the only one able to get through to him.

Billy knows that David's not his biological dad but he doesn't know the whole back story. Perhaps it's time…

"Leave it with David, he will sort it all out, I know he will," she reassures me, patting my arm.

I smile and get back to peeling potatoes. We need to get a wriggle on if we're to do this prep before the children wake.

*

We're sat in the living room, all dressed in our finest Christmas jumpers. The fire in the Inglenook fireplace is roaring courtesy of Grandpa Kyd giving it a good blasting and the children are hopping around, excitedly showing off their gifts. Davy is on my knee, bouncing about happily. He seems to have taken well to formula so I'm letting my boobs dry up now, I've decided. It's time, once and for all, to have my body back as my own!

David leans over from the other side of the sofa we're observing from, asking, "Do you want your gift yet?"

"What? I told you not to get me anything."

"Don't be daft."

He puts a little box on my lap and beckons for me to pass him Davy.

With a slight scowl, I unwrap the present, pulling out a jewellery box.

Inside is an eternity ring with two white gold swans encrusted in diamonds.

"Oh my god," I breathe, flush with emotion, my eyes drawing tears immediately, "David!"

"Do you like it?"

"It's ridiculously extravagant and I love it!"

We didn't get wedding rings for our second wedding. I still have my original rings but they rest against my heart most days, hidden beneath my clothes on a chain.

I slide the swans down my wedding finger and admire them.

"It was engraved," he says, trying to see past me through Davy's waving arms, "did you see?"

"Oh… no." I pull the ring back off even though I don't want to and read the engraving: *For life.*

A lump in my throat, I swing my arms around him, kissing him on the lips with eager tenderness.

"Ewww, yack," squawks Marissa, the absolute spit of Rachel. Unfortunately however, she has my attitude.

"What is it? Let me see what you got?" asks Rachel.

I show her the ring and her hands fly to her cheeks. "Good golly!"

"I told him not to get me anything."

"And I told her not to get me anything…" David shrugs.

I pretend I haven't. "Sorry… I thought you were serious?"

He looks downcast. "You're happy, that's all that matters."

David gives his attention to Davy, blowing bubbles at our youngest. Davy's presents haven't been wrapped, they're just sitting in the nursery, ready to play with whenever. Not that he really needs any more toys, not with all that he inherited from his elder siblings…

I rummage under the natural fir tree, trying to remember where I hid David's gift. I buried it deep on purpose.

Pulling out presents, I mediate between Lucinda and

Marissa still squabbling, both of them unwrapping at the speed of light to try and beat each other to the finish. I bought them exactly the same things so there's no argument.

I notice Billy's one present of a new laptop has disappeared and so has he. That was his only present because that was all he wanted.

I look around the room and notice he's nowhere near the tree, nowhere in the room in fact.

After making a pile of things we've got for Rachel, my dad, and a couple of token gifts for Julie and Dr Kers, I summon the courage to slither on my belly under the bowel of the tree and reach for David's hidden gift. He has no idea I got him this and I know he hates surprises.

"Oh… it looks like Santa came for David after all!" I yell from where I'm buried under all the greenery.

David drags me by the legs from beneath the humongous tree we had craned in and chuckles as I present him with a small parcel.

"'To David, from Santa', it says, I guess you better open it then."

He shakes his head and I smile over his shoulder at Rachel, holding Davy.

"What did you get him, Ade?" my dad says, "a guide to good manners?"

My father and David have a very special relationship… a club perhaps even… of constant good-natured put downs and escapes to the pub when family life becomes all too much and the bath becomes my home.

David seats himself with me in the leather couch and rips off the paper. When he gets to the object within, he sits back and stares at it.

It's a First Edition of *Ulysses*, his favourite book. It cost me a fortune, but he's worth every penny. I can tell he's shocked.

When he opens the cover and sees it's even signed, I think he might be about to actually cry.

"I spent a lot on your ring, but this… I think we most likely bought our first house for less than what this cost."

"Well I think it's an investment," I argue, "I think this will sit very nicely in a glass case in the study, reminding you that legacies do last forever, and all you need is a little belief."

"You've shut David up. You actually shut him up," my father says, "look, he's gob smacked."

Dad leans down to kiss my cheek and lets me know, "I'll check on the turkey. Don't want it drying out. Probably needs another baste." He winks and lets me know he's very proud of how I've done this year. I sold one of my offshore investments to buy the book for David. £20,000 became a hundred times more and then, it bought a book. Not any ordinary book.

"I can't believe–"

Billy stomps into the room, barging into the emotional scene with the words, "You put the child locks on! I'm not a baby! I can't access anything on the internet. I mean… you may as well not have bothered!"

His fury compounds mine and I bite my lip hard to stop myself reacting.

David looks from me to Billy, giving his stepson a level glare. "We'll take it back, then."

"No–I–it's just–" His words become tongue-tied.

David passes me the book to take care of and walks across the room to Billy, hands in his pockets, his calm façade no doubt alarming our son.

David's only ever calm when he's actually livid inside.

The punch bag in the basement knows when David's been livid as do the rest of us. His body winds tight whenever he goes down there and returns ever tighter.

"For your information William, fifteen is the age of a child. In fact sixteen, seventeen, eighteen even in some countries, is the age of a child. In America people don't drink legally until they're twenty-one. Now you can't smoke until you're eighteen. So as you can tell, you're still very much in the bracket of being a child and is that outraged expression any way to thank your mother for a gift she didn't have to buy for you?"

"Thank you," he mumbles, head down.

"If you want to buy your own, fully adult laptop then get a paper round and buy your own fully adult laptop. Or better yet, get a business of your own like Mum has, then you can live like an adult, with access to all the disgusting depravities available on the net."

I look David straight in the eye when he says that. We share a knowing look. Yep, we're never letting our kids on the internet. Never ever.

Billy begins to turn from the room.

"And another thing… Grandma tells us you've been fooling around in your bedroom again."

"I haven't, we were only–"

David zips his mouth. "I don't care what happened, or what didn't happen. You must ask us before inviting some-one to stay over. If you don't ask permission and we catch Henry in your bedroom again, I will freeze your allowance until the next century, ban you off the internet, make you walk the five miles to school everyday and basically, I will stop you from enjoying every last liberty you enjoy under this roof."

"You're just being homophobic!"

For a split second, I see David's fist clench, as though he would like to punch Billy – but can't. Billy wants us to do things like that, but we have to fight against it all the time. He goads us to react, to retaliate, to match the bitter hate he feels in his heart over something that hasn't even happened yet – and we have to constantly fight against it, together.

I feel as though Christmas might be ruined if David doesn't nip this in the bud and quickly.

"What's going on?" my father asks as he steps into the room.

David folds his arms. "Billy had a friend over without permission. Oh and he doesn't like the laptop his mother gave him for Christmas."

My father's eyes cross. "What? Do you know what I got for Christmas all throughout my teenage years?"

Billy shrugs.

"I got an orange in a sock, a new pair of pants, a packet of sweets and a new deck of cards."

"Nah, you didn't."

"I did so," my father replies, "I wasn't born made of money. Be more grateful."

Billy shrugs again, shifting his feet into the carpet, a move I saw Marcus make a million times. Shame often hung his head for a while until the trouble causer inside him reared up once more.

"I've recently put a lot of money in trust for you kids but I can easily take it back again."

"What, money?" Billy mumbles.

"Lots of money," Dad replies, "which you'll get when you're twenty-one, like your mother did, but you have to pass your exams, either have a job or be in university, be doing well and responsible, otherwise I will cut you off. You could learn a lot from your mother. Do you think she got everything she got from looking up porn on the internet…"

I keep my lips firmly pressed together!

"…no, she did hard graft, something you could learn a thing or two about. How about an internship with me. Unpaid, mind. But maybe if you're good, we'll see…"

Billy's eyes brighten. "Really?"

"Why not? You should have asked me sooner!"

Billy runs to his granddad, cuddling him. "Thanks, Granddad."

"You'll have to start small like everyone does. Making coffee. Buying newspapers, couple of days after school every week. You need to do well at school, Billy. It's your best chance. Listen to your parents, they did well at school."

Billy pouts. "But I'm not like Dad, all academic. And I'm not like Mum, really good with numbers. I like computers. I like that sort of stuff."

I look at David because neither of us have had a good conversation with Billy in months. Maybe he hates that we've brought another kid into his life…

Anyway I think it's more likely that he just finds it easier to open up to his grandfather…

"Let's talk as we baste the turkey some more," Dad says, taking Billy out of the room.

Marissa and Lucinda have piled up their stuff and are both looking at me with fierce glares.

"Mum, I got everything she got, but just in pink."

"And I got everything she got, but just in purple."

I smile. "Aren't you both lucky?"

"Mum!" Marissa turns her lip up. "We've got all the

same stuff. That's boring!"

"No it's not, it's diplomatic," David says, "we both know you'd fight if you had different stuff."

The girls look at one another, giving each other the eye. They fold their arms like their father and Marissa goads her elder sister, "Last one upstairs with all their stuff is a rotten egg!"

They start chasing up the stairs and for just a few moments, we have a bit of peace. Rachel and Julie are in the corner nursery area playing with Davy and Dr Kers is out in the hall discussing a surgery he may have to leave the house for later today…

Laying back in the sofa together, we cuddle each other tight. Admiring my ring, I mumble, "I love it. Do you love yours?"

"I'm scared shitless of it. I know how much they're worth!"

I whisper in his ear, "It's so hard with Billy sometimes. I don't feel like I'm good enough or that I ever will be."

David caresses my hair. "He doesn't know the facts, though. I think it's time."

I swallow. "Me too."

"Tonight, I'll get him on his own."

"You'll do it? But–"

He puts an index finger over my mouth. "Hush, Adrienne."

The girls come spiralling back into the room, brunette plaits flying, big dresses flashing in the air behind them. "I'm gonna beat you! I'm gonna beat you!"

"You are not!" Lucinda yells, and they take more from the room, arms carrying bag loads of presents to their den upstairs.

"Be bloody careful on those stairs!" I yell. "I am not going to A&E again this year. I've been enough times already!"

I sigh as they chase back upstairs, burrowing into David's jumper, thinking back to when I had his rather delicious cock in my mouth.

*

David's been upstairs for an hour or two. The girls are in bed, exhausted from their marathon unwrapping and playing sessions today. I'm sure they had bets on who could play longer and better! Their competitiveness is commendable but I sometimes wish they didn't take after me. I'm holding a glass of red, luxuriating in the end of the day. The dish-washer is doing its final load and my father, Julie, Rachel and Dr Kers all left a while ago, their tummies touching table before they went. Dr Kers has to perform surgery tonight. He didn't drink at all today but I still can't help but think I overfed him to lethargy. Maybe the feast will keep him going… I did pour coffee in abundance for him before he left.

My feet up on a pouffe and all the lights of the tree glitt-ering against the dim room, I smile. It's been an exhausting day but nevertheless worthwhile. It's difficult not to think about what's going on upstairs because I can't help but think Billy will take it all very badly once he learns the truth. I've tried to put it off for years, I've told myself it will never help him to know, and yet he has to know. He has to know that the reason I sometimes can't bear to look at him isn't because he isn't wanted or that I never loved him. It's because he is so much like his father, it scares me. I'm just human. I've tried to teach all my children the same but Billy has always been more difficult than the others. Granted, Davy is still a baby but my girls have always been easier, immediately cajoled with cuddles and kisses and sweet treats on occasion. Billy's always been a very deep boy, very contemplative, almost too quiet for my liking. I often wonder what he's thinking.

I can't bear this waiting so I wander upstairs, leaving my glass where it is.

Tiptoeing down the corridor, I make it to Billy's door and hang around outside.

I hear them talking quietly and Billy explains, "I see how warm she is with my sisters and it hurts, I can't explain it… it's just that I know she feels differently about them. She's closer with them and when you were gone that time, do you know how that made me feel? I felt completely alone when you were gone. How do I know you won't be gone again?"

I hear desperation in his tone. I know now he's just been rebelling against us because he doesn't know any other way of trying to tell us he's worried and hurt.

"Why would I go? Where would I go?" David asks.

"I don't know but I saw in your office a letter with a job offer or something… I don't know… are you going to take it?"

"What?" David demands.

"You were on the phone! I heard you going on about–"

"Yes, yes, okay. I might be having one of my books made into a film and we may have to go on set! I want to help produce it and do the screenplay."

"Oh my god. What's the story about…?"

"Well… it's about a woman who's trying to escape an abusive relationship. It's loosely based on someone I knew.

The only way out, is for her to kill the man."

"What?"

"Yep."

"That's awful. What does the man do to her?"

"Stamps on her body, smashes her head into walls. Hurts her very badly indeed. The book centres on whether she's guilty. In the end, the evidence isn't enough to condemn her. She gets off because she was protecting her child."

We've only ever told Billy that his father went away and is never coming back. We didn't tell him how he met his end.

I killed him…

"I've spoken to Grandma and she says you can stay with her while we're out of the country, just while you finish your GCSEs."

"Couldn't I stay with Grandpa instead? Julie makes the best cooked breakfasts."

"Either way, as long as he's okay with it."

"So you and Mum aren't splitting up? What about her job? The other night I thought you were going away on like one of those last-ditch nights you hear other kid's parents going on about… like to make or break their marriages or whatever. You'd both been so tired and crabby lately."

"I'm sorry but that's what comes with being a parent. You'll be happy to know that the only thing our night away taught us was that we need to visit the doctor to get me the snip."

Billy laughs, the same laugh Marcus and Luca had.

I live in fear everyday that one day he might snap and turn into one of them, but I have hope. I have hope that David has been a better influence on him than they ever would have been.

"You can come visit the set. We'll be shooting in a few different countries. Your sisters will be schooled on set, the film company has really good international tutors for the kids of people making films. I love your mother very much and I have absolutely no intention of ever leaving her, she's my heart and soul. I know we fight and argue sometimes but that's what adults do. We fight and then it's out in the open, and gone. That's better than bottling it all up."

"I guess so…"

"Billy, I'm not gonna make promises about the future. None of us know what may happen. That's the unpredictability of life. But… we all need to stick together. It's the only thing that matters."

I see through the gap in the door that Billy is nodding. "It's pretty sweet your story is gonna be made into a film. It sounds raw as well, like it came from that black imagination of yours they're always going on about in the reviews."

David smiles wryly. "The truth is stranger than fiction."

David stands up and Billy gets in bed with his new laptop, about to play on a game, his earphones at the ready.

"Thanks for caring, you know? Even though you're not my real dad."

Billy has the tact of a high-speed train sometimes. "I've been there since you were two. I'm your only dad."

"I know but I also know I don't take after you two, either of you… it's difficult. Not to mention being gay. I know I'm a disappointment."

"Have we ever said that?"

I take my chance to escape and overhear Billy say, "No, but…"

I tiptoe back downstairs and into the living room once more, picking up the long stem of my bulbous wine glass. I take a long, slow drink, swirling the spicy liquid around my mouth.

David enters the room some minutes later, seating himself beside me.

Sighing, he reveals, “He thinks he’s so grown up, which is half the problem.”

“I suppose he had to grow up quick in some ways. You died and came back to life! It’s got to have had an impact.”

“Listen, Ade,” he says, taking my hands, “he’s not ready to know the truth. In fact I don’t think he ever will be. It’s something us two will have to cope with together. You know?”

I turn and face him, our knees touching. “I overheard some of what you were saying up there and I agree.”

“The truth is unimaginable for him. He’s just a kid.”

“And yet what I went through happens all the time…” I turn and stare into the fire.

“Yes but he’s very much a child inside, whether he wants to admit it or not.”

“I know,” I accept, even though it’s hard to. “I just don’t want him to think I love him any less. It’s just that it’s more difficult to love him, but I love him just as much as the others. It’s also that when you were dead, David… it was so bad between me and him. I shut down and he hated me for it. He still doesn’t understand why I shut down sometimes. I don’t want to be like this but I can’t help it. You know I discuss this with my therapist and we’re trying but it’s such an inbuilt defence mechanism, I don’t know if I will ever get past it.”

“Come here,” he asks, tugging me close, my knees on his lap. He brushes his nose to mine and whispers, “It’ll all be okay. Now kiss me.”

So I kiss him.

When I pull back, he's wearing a filthy grin.

"What?" I squint.

"When you were laid up and I started calling you bunny, I saw a little thing in a shop once and I tucked it away for a rainy day."

"A rainy day, eh?"

"Yes…"

"And…"

"It's a little bunny tail attached to a little bunny plug and there's a little bunny collar with a little bunny lead."

I burst out laughing, then bury my face in his warm, strong neck.

"God you're a hound."

"About to chase my bunny…"

I run away, as fast as I can, my fierce man hot on my heels.

Before we enter the bedroom, I halt him with a hand on his chest.

"Wait, what should I call you tonight? Master? Daddy… sir?"

He delivers one of his famous lopsided grins. "Just call me Sir Pimpmaster Daddy."

"Can't I have something shorter?" I deadpan, but I have to work hard to keep a straight face.

"Call me David," he says, throwing me up over his shoulder, locking us inside the bedroom together. I manage to contain my squeal as he tosses me onto the bed, but when he produces the lead, collar and butt plug, I can't help but laugh the house down.

While he's ripping off my clothes, I beg, "Just promise me that after we're done, we'll curl up together and you'll read to me from a book like we always do on Christmas night."

He looks up from what he's doing. "After I'm done with you, you'll need matchsticks to keep your eyes open if you aren't already asleep."

I smile. "Okay, then."

"Can of worms, Ade… you've opened a fucking can of worms!"

TEN

January 3rd

I walk into his office, knowing he's flabbergasted. He wasn't expecting me here first day back, but I'm here. Although… I am wearing jeans and a throw-on blouse.

"Adrienne, I don't have long. You should have made an appointment."

"I just need five minutes," I tell him.

This morning I woke up and instead of getting to work in the home study, I got into my Range Rover and drove straight here.

"Okay…"

"I've made a decision to go with David on his next work commitment. Which means I'll need time off, a sabbatical or something."

He looks surprised, leaning forward across the desk, his hands together. "What's that involve?"

"One of his books is being turned into a film."

"Really?"

"Hmm-mmm. He's semi-producing it and writing the script. He's really not taking any chances. He doesn't want it to become all Hollywood-ised, you know? All the dirt washed away. He wants the truth to be out there. It's a gritty book."

"Oh, which one?"

"It's not been published yet," I lie.

"Wow. Well, I think you're making a mistake leaving." He's not apologetic for his non-apologetic demeanour. He makes absolutely no excuses for himself.

I wonder if Kat likes the bastard in the bedroom, but nowhere else…

"Why do you think I'm making a mistake?"

"You're very good at what you do, plus you know I can't just give you a sabbatical. You had maternity leave this tax year already."

I stand from my seat. "Then I guess I resign. I was willing to let you keep my skills for a little give and take… but…"

"Wait, wait, hold up–"

I wait, patiently.

He walks round the desk to look me in the eye.

"You know it's not how it works around here, Adrienne."

"You mean that audits continually prove I'm the most efficient worker yet when I want a little something back, I get nada."

He licks his lips, fighting a losing battle. "I can enquire, but–"

"The defeat in your eyes tells me everything I already know. You won't fight for me, like you won't fight for the happiness you crave but are too scared to ask for…"

He frowns, his aged face crumpling. "What are you talking about?"

"Kat… and that baby."

He goes silent and expressionless, then looks at the floor. "I thought there was at least one person left who didn't know about my cesspit of a love life."

"Even I know, so it must be bad. This is the first time I came to the office in six months…"

He points at my chair for me to sit back down and we stare across the table at one another.

After a few minutes he says, "I had the snip so I know… you know? I mean, I thought I wanted kids but Kat never did and I had the snip and then I thought I could get it reversed so I just told Mrs Pietersen to go and get knocked up, which she did. But… it's fucked up. She's so young and depending on me but she doesn't really love me and the only woman who does really love me is Kat."

I shake my head at him. "You should fight for her. She's one hell of a woman."

"I'm too much of a coward. She got rid of me once before."

"Yes because you let her down when it counted. And why was that?"

He lifts his eyes. "I shut people out."

I reach for a notelet on his desk and a pen, writing down the therapist I use.

"I shut people out too. It nearly cost me my life, if you can believe it. Dr Rubenstein helps. She's amazing. Just try not to fuck her, although she is like eighty, I think. It might just be the long silver hair, but she has wisdom… let me tell you."

He stares at me, searching my face. "But you're so perfect, you and David. You adore one another."

"We do, but it's never simple when it comes to real love. You fear losing it so you try to break it, you try to hurt the other person because you're scared of getting hurt first…"

He fingers the paper in his hand, letting his guard down. "I was with a woman many years ago. She got rid of my baby without telling me and ran off with someone else shortly afterwards. It left me like this."

I give him a sympathetic smile and rise from my chair. We shake hands across the table.

"I'll work my notice and call you when we get back. That's if I haven't discovered a vineyard to run or a lake to live by in the interim."

He smiles wryly. "I envy you."

"Why?"

"You have someone who loves you no matter what."

I shrug. "I can be ugly, it's just he loves the ugly bits as well."

"Ugly isn't a word to go in the same sentence as you."

I smile, a smile full of regret and retrospect. I've been labouring for these people for a few years now, just a little scared to spread my wings and fly.

I have to admit, a new chapter will be scary – but nice.

"Goodbye, Mika."

"Farewell, Adrienne. Enjoy life."

"Oh… I think I will, dear. I really will."

I wink, then I'm gone.

Oh, but I think I will…

ABOUT THE AUTHOR

Sarah knew from about the age of eight that whatever she did in life, it would no doubt involve words.

After achieving a degree in English, the world of journalism almost swallowed her whole but thankfully a period of maternity leave gave her that small window of opportunity to write creatively whenever her baby slept, which was thankfully often.

Since then, Sarah has taken up editing as a career but still writes everyday too. *The Contract* is her fifteenth novel and Sarah writes everything from sci-fi, to paranormal, erotica and romance. She will admit her favourite genre to write is suspense.

You can find Sarah on all the usual social networks but she favours Twitter, where you can find her on this handle: @SarahMichelleLy

16162287R00076

Printed in Poland
by Amazon Fulfillment
Poland Sp. z o.o., Wrocław